DELTA

DISCOVERY

a novel of early T-Space™

Alastair Mayer

Mabash Books

DELTA PAVONIS: DISCOVERY

For announcements about other T-Space books and special offers, sign up for Alastair Mayer's newsletter at http://www.alastairmayer.net/

A Mabash Books original.

First printing, September 2021

Mabash Books, Centennial, Colorado

Hardcover: ISBN-13: 978-1-948188-272
Trade Paper ISBN-13: 978-1-948188-289

DELTA PAVONIS: DISCOVERY

a novel of early T-Space™

Contents

DELTA PAVONIS:

DISCOVERY

a novel of early T-Space™

Part I - Plans

Chapter I: The Idea

Queen's University campus, Kingston, Ontario (2077)
Paul Fabron sat on the grass at Breakwater Park, leaning back against a tree, enjoying the unusually warm late-April day. Other students were enjoying it in their own ways, and one in particular caught his eye. He was enjoying the sight—her long blonde hair loose in the light breeze, her figure trim and athletic—when she suddenly darted toward him and reached to grab a Frisbee out of the air in front of his face.

"Sorry," she said, smiling.

"*Pas de problème,*" Paul replied, but she had already turned to toss it back to her friend. *Oh well.* Sometimes his accent—Parisian, not Quebecois—encouraged further conversation, but he had to be going soon anyway. As if to emphasize that thought, the omniphone on his wrist chimed a reminder.

He rose and crossed the nearby King Street to Leonard Field, the quad sandwiched between Morris and Gordon-Brockington Halls, then cut between Morris and Brant Hall, crossing Albert Street at Stuart. From there, he went through the parking lot to the back door of Stirling Hall, the Physics building.

He made his way up the stairs to the main floor, then around the curved corridor—the building was roughly circular, rumored to accommodate a cyclotron in the basement, but as far as Paul knew, it was because of the large wedge-shaped lecture theaters. He continued to the north-east foyer, where his housemate and fellow engineering student, Rick McDonald, waited for him.

"Well?" Paul said, "What did you find out?"

"Let's walk," Rick said. "I'll tell you on the way."

They joined the stream of students on Bader Lane—a historical quirk had sited the physics building amid residence halls, and it was nearing supper time. The crowd thinned out as they rounded the Art Centre and headed north up University.

"So? Is it something you didn't want overheard?"

"Not quite that dramatic," Rick admitted. "Mostly, I didn't want to hang around talking when we could be on our way home. I'm hungry."

Paul muttered something in French, then said, "So what *did* you find out?"

"Professor Kercheval does indeed have a contact on the fifty-meter telescope team, a former student in fact. And yes, they're doing an exoplanet survey of all the G- and K-type stars within warp ship range. Actually, within ten parsecs, so a bit more than what current ships are capable of."

The fifty-meter instrument was a newly launched orbital telescope, in theory capable of imaging the surfaces of planets light years away, albeit in limited detail. It might make out the continents on Kakuloa or Sawyer's World, at Alpha Centauri, but beyond that, anything Earth-sized would be only a few pixels across.

"*Fantastique!* And?"

"And that's all he could tell me, or at least was willing to. I'll have to speak to his contact myself to see if I can get any more out of him."

They crossed Union Street, still heading north on University. Rick glanced across at the University Centre. "The Underground is going be busy tonight, what with classes over." That was the student-run nightclub in the Centre's basement.

"Classes, perhaps, although we still have exams. But no doubt you're right. How starving are you? We could eat here." The Centre had several food outlets.

"Nah, let's get home. Mary will want to hear."

"Hear what? You have little to tell her."

"What about you? Any luck on finding us a starship?"

Paul just smiled. "I can't tell you now. I thought you said Mary would want to hear."

"*Merde*," muttered Rick.

"*Très bien*. Your accent is improving."

∞ ∞ ∞

Student house, Kingston, a week earlier

Mary Kalvak guessed from Paul's exasperated look that whoever was on the other end of his omniphone was family. His next words confirmed it.

"*Oui, Papa.*" A pause, then "*Oui, oui, Papa. Mais—*"

Mary grinned to herself. She had never met Paul Fabron's father, but if half of what the news media said about him was true, he was a domineering, focused, no-nonsense man. On the plus side, those qualities had helped *Monsieur* Fabron build up a multi-billion-euro engineering company. Technically, he was also their landlord; he had bought the house, probably at far beyond market price, to give Paul both a place to live, and to gain experience managing property. To hear Paul tell it, his father hadn't so much let him escape France to attend college here at Queen's University, but had virtually ordered him to. As Paul had paraphrased it, "if it was good enough for Elon Musk, it's good enough for you." That Paul's mother was Canadian may also have had something to do with it.

"*Mais—*" Paul seemed to be on the losing side of an argument, but that was the way most of the infrequent phone calls with his father went. "*D'accord. Au revoir!*" He slapped his omniphone off, muttering "*Merde!*" under his breath. He looked up and noticed Mary.

"Oh, hi," he said, a bit sheepish. "How long have you been there?"

"Just long enough to know that your father was doing most of the talking, and it was something you're not happy about. Problems?"

Paul shrugged. "The usual. He wants me to get more hands-on experience running the company, so he's threatening to post me to one of his overseas branches for the summer."

"Only threatening? So, what do you have to do to get out of it?" Mary found it a little hard to be sympathetic. She'd worked for several years both during and after high school to be able to afford college, and while she had loved her work, as a bush pilot in the Canadian north, she wanted to move beyond that.

"Find something equivalent on my own. Which is fine with me, but—"

"But the problem is finding something that both interests you and would be challenging enough to please your father."

"*Oui, exactement.* Is that experience talking?"

Mary sighed. "Yes, but from my mother, actually."

The front door opened and Rick entered, tossing his backpack on the faded couch. Upon seeing Mary's and Paul's glum expressions, he said lightheartedly, "Hi honey, I'm home."

∞ ∞ ∞

"Classes are almost over," Rick had said. "Why are you all looking so glum?"

"Paul just got off the phone with his father," Mary said.

"Ah. Say no more."

The door opened again as two more of their housemates, Fred and Suzette, arrived home.

"Hi guys," Fred said. "Suzette and I were thinking of heading over to The Underground for a drink. Who's joining us?"

"Are you kidding?" Rick said. "Final exams are coming up, and I have a project to finish. I don't have time to celebrate."

"That's what you get for partying during the year instead of studying," Suzette said. She was being facetious; Rick rarely partied.

Mary wasn't amused either. "Oh, piss off." She was a few years older than the others, her straight black hair and a slightly dumpy, Asian look contrasting with Suzette's red-haired brush cut. That didn't bother Mary; any guys to whom it made a difference were too shallow for her anyway. "Some of us had to work to cover living expenses too, you know."

Paul looked over at her. "You went flying almost every weekend, was that work?"

"Well, I got paid for it. Nobody said I wasn't allowed to enjoy it." In fact, it wasn't always enjoyable. Most of the flying had been for the university's sport parachute club, and the routine of boarding a crew of jumpers, taking them up a few thousand meters, dealing with them piling out of the aircraft, and then landing to do it all again did get a bit old. Flying the old rattletrap aircraft the club could afford, with a seat only for the pilot and flying with the door off, wasn't exactly a treat at the best of times. Sometimes she got lucky and had a charter to Ottawa or Toronto, and got to rack up some time in something more elegant, and at better pay rates. Other times, since she had an instructor's rating, she filled in at the local flying school. Sometimes she missed her time as a bush pilot up north, but only sometimes.

"Speaking of work, what are everyone's plans for the summer?" Rick asked. "Retaking the classes we flunked?"

The others took it as a joke. Rick was more intelligent than he sometimes acted. "Very funny," Paul said. "My father is after me to get involved in the business more."

"More?" Fred asked. "Aren't you already like running a division or something?"

"Hardly that. More like apprenticing in that role. I get to read all the reports and write up recommendations for decisions that have already been made, just to see if I would have made better or worse choices."

"So, you're like doing the work of a business major without getting the credit," Fred said. "Tell me again why you're in engineering?"

"As my father puts it, 'it's easier to teach an engineer accounting than it is to teach an accountant engineering.' Fabron Industries is an engineering company first, and he wants to keep it that way."

"He's got a point," Suzette said. "Look at all the big technology companies of the last century that went to hell after the bean-counters took over. Ones that got their start with electronics and computers, or aircraft, or—"

"Don't you start," Paul said. "And I don't disagree. Except that what he wants me to actually do is more accounting than engineering or science."

"What do you want to do?" Mary asked.

"Not sit in an office at one of Papa's companies shuffling data files and reports, that's for certain. I'd like something more adventurous. Business is starting to boom on Kakuloa; perhaps try my hand at starting something up there."

"Kakuloa? You mean the planet at Alpha Centauri? I thought the pharmaceutical companies had all that nailed down."

"No," Fred said, "it's not just them. There's a huge resort at Kakuloa City. Beaches, casinos, you name it. It's not even officially open yet, and it's already booked months in advance."

Rick looked at Paul. "You want to open a casino?"

"No, of course not. There's a mining operation too, and all kinds of support businesses. It's a boom town, or rather, planet."

"Haven't you missed the window?" Suzette asked. "First mover advantage was a few years ago, when the *Endeavour* went back. If you really want to make it big, you need to find a new planet."

"It's a big galaxy. That shouldn't be too hard." Paul said with a grin.

"Right, what's the current range on a starship? Ten, maybe twelve light years? And the galaxy is how big?" Mary said.

"Something over fifty thousand light years across," Rick said. He was studying engineering physics, but also doing a minor in astronomy and astrophysics. "But there are over five hundred sun-like stars within a hundred light years. That's just G-type stars. There are more if you count K-type like Kakuloa's sun, or Epsilon Eridani."

Paul looked at him. "How many of those have planets?"

"Nobody knows the exact number, but probably most of them. Of the eight G- and K-type stars within a dozen light years, at least six have planets. We're not sure about 61 Cygni, it might. We know it has a dust ring."

"So, seventy-five percent. How many of those six stars have *terraformed* planets?" Eight years earlier, the first Alpha Centauri expedition had brought back the startling news that two planets in that system had been terraformed, with life imported from Earth, millions of years earlier. There had been no indication of how or by whom, or what.

"That we know of? Four. Well, three, actually, since I was including Earth. But the other two systems haven't been visited yet, last I heard, so three for three, maybe four for four."

The number surprised Paul. That made it virtually certain that any sun-like star with planets had one that was terraformed. Whoever the Terraformers were, those tens of millions of years ago, they had been busy. It also meant that there was an incredible opportunity for early explorers.

"Probably just as well that nobody can claim a planet," Fred said.

"Even if they did, how would they defend it? What's to stop someone landing on the opposite side of Sawyer's World from the capital and setting up shop?"

"The Treaty of Alpha Centauri and the *UDT* Space Force, for starters," Paul said. He had some familiarity with space law; Fabron Industries had substantial activity in space.

"The *Union de Terre* has a Space Force?" Mary said.

"It can call on member nations for support. In practice, it's mostly limited to the space between here and the Moon. Nobody is worried about pirates any more than Christopher Columbus or Jacques Cartier were," Paul explained. "Anyway, Sawyer's World is open to settlement. You have to agree to their covenants, but they aren't very strict.

"But this is all beside the point," he continued. "Nobody is going to claim a planet, not sovereignty, anyway. The Outer

Space Treaty and the *UDT* won't allow it, and you wouldn't need to. Centauri Pharmaceuticals hasn't claimed Kakuloa, they just have an exclusive right to market products derived from Kakuloan biochemistry."

"Oh," Suzette said. "So, it's like a mining claim; it gives exclusive right to the minerals, but not unrelated uses."

Paul nodded. "*Oui*, and the *UDT* member nations *can* enforce that, because the only market is on Earth."

"At least for now," Fred said. He seemed to be getting bored with the conversation.

"It will be a long time before the off-planet market approaches even one percent of the Earth market," Paul said.

"So instead of finding and claiming a planet, you only need to find a planet and claim exclusive marketing rights for its products. Easy, eh?" Rick said, his sarcasm obvious.

"Look at the history of the Age of Exploration," Paul said. "Companies were formed to do exactly that: the East India Company, the Hudson's Bay Company . . . and that one's still around, although it's changed its name a few times. Didn't they celebrate their 400th anniversary a few years ago? Many others."

Mary, who had mostly been holding back from the conversation, piped up. "So, we create an exploration company, somehow get hold of a starship, and go find a new planet and claim exclusive merchandising rights to it?"

Paul wasn't sure how a purely hypothetical discussion had changed to something 'we' would do, but he was rapidly warming to the idea.

He nodded. "*Oui*. Forming a company is easy; I've done it before. Claiming exclusive rights, well, I have heard that there is a plan in place to simplify the granting of patents for such things."

"Patents?"

"Perhaps that isn't the right term, but some sort of time-limited, exclusive license like a patent. It's to simplify commercial expansion in space. I'd have to look up the details; I don't know if it passed yet."

"What about a ship, eh?" Rick said. "And finding a planet?"

"I think finding a planet, or rather, a potential planet, comes first. Isn't that what telescopes are for? You're the astronomer. What about it?"

"There aren't any telescopes good enough to tell if a planet is terraformed or not at interstellar distances," Rick said. "Sometimes we can estimate the mass, and maybe tell something by spectroscopic analysis, depending on how far away it is and how clear a picture we can get, but that's it."

"What about the new fifty-meter telescope?" Paul wondered. The monstrous space telescope, the biggest optical telescope yet, had finished assembly in high Earth orbit some months back. So far, very few pictures from it had been published.

"That's *with* that telescope, but it's only been up there for a little while. Don't expect any results to be published for a year or so."

"*Mais non*. Who said we have to wait for results to be published? Surely within the astronomical community, preliminary results are known?"

Rick looked at Paul suspiciously. "What are you saying?"

"You know it takes a while for findings to get analyzed, written up as a paper, the paper to go through peer review, and finally published. The raw information is available at the first step of that, *n'est-ce pas*?"

"Things are a little quicker than that in astronomy, with preprints and an alert network for sudden events like supernovae, but sure, if you knew someone on the observing team, and they managed to schedule time to look at what you were interested in, you might hear about it early. So what?"

"Just brainstorming. The most efficient way to find a new planet is *not* to hop in a starship and start randomly going from star to star. It's to look and see what stars have potential candidates first. A good telescope helps."

"Well, of course," Rick said.

"And a survey of nearer sun-like stars surely wouldn't take very long."

"That depends on where planets are in their orbits. It doesn't help if a planet is behind the star, or directly in front of it. It would be lost in the glare. But we have a lot of data on exoplanet orbits and masses already, from their gravity. I guess you're right."

"Wait a minute, guys," Mary said. "Is this just hypothetical? I mean, Paul, you're not actually thinking of setting up an exploration company to do this. Are you?" There was a note of hopefulness in that last question.

"Why not?" Paul said. "My father wants me to get experience running a company this summer. He should be careful what he wishes for."

"But . . . how much can it accomplish in one summer? Four months? For an interstellar expedition? Assuming we even find a destination?"

"It takes only a few days to get to Alpha Centauri. Why not? They are building a lot of starships for the Kakuloa trade."

"This is ridiculous," Fred said, rising from his seat. "I don't care how rich your family is, Paul, they're not going to give you a starship. I've had enough. I'm going over to The Underground for a drink. Who's with me?"

"Sure, I already said so." Suzette said. "Rick, Mary?"

"Maybe later," Rick said. Mary just shook her head.

"*Eh bien*," Paul said as they left. "I guess I won't be inviting *them*."

Rick studied his expression. "Don't tease, Paul. You know this is the kind of thing I want to do. Are you serious? Do you really think you can get a starship?"

The more Paul considered it, the more convinced he became. Worst case, if the business never got off the ground, perhaps even literally, he could still convince his father it had been a worthwhile learning experience. He would need to raise the money for a ship, but a charter should be possible. Perhaps he could even buy a lightly used one and resell it after the expedition. Such things were done with aircraft and oceangoing ships, so it should be possible with starships. He knew some people he could reach out to. "Yes," he said firmly, "I am."

"In that case," Mary said, "you'll need a pilot. I'm available."

"*Un moment*, we don't even have a destination or a ship yet. And you're not spaceship certified." He paused. She often surprised him. She just might be qualified. "Are you?"

"No," she admitted, "but I could be by the time you're ready. I have the flight hours. I only need to pass a test on space traffic regulations and get a few hours of checkout time. Spaceships are all automated anyway. The pilot is really a systems manager."

"But what if we don't find a destination? Or it isn't terraformed? The company will lose money." He wanted her to know what she was getting into.

"Then hire me as an employee. I don't have anything to invest to be a partner anyway. That way, the company pays for my training as well as my time." She fixed him in her gaze. "Or were you not really serious after all?"

Paul looked at her defiant stare. He wasn't about to back down now. He knew he could arrange a preliminary round of funding, even if it was just family friends humoring him, although he hoped it wouldn't come to that. Paying Mary a salary and covering her spacecraft flight training wouldn't cost much; the real costs would come with obtaining a ship and outfitting the expedition. Yes, he could do this.

He looked at her. "All right. You're hired. Congratulations, employee number two."

"Two?"

"I'm employee number one, of course. Although I'll only take a dollar in salary and the rest as profit sharing. Speaking of, I'll set up a profit-sharing plan for employees, too."

"You're going to need an engineer, and an astronomer," Rick said.

"You're probably right," Paul said. "Do you know one?"

"Hey!"

"I'm joking. You can be employee number three. But before we go any further, I need to pull a business plan and the articles of incorporation together and make this all legal."

"What are you going to call this company?" Mary asked. "The Interstellar Company?"

"That's a bit broad, *n'est-ce pas*? For now, it will be a numbered corporation. When we figure out a destination, I'll file a doing-business-as some more meaningful name."

"If you say so. I'll be right back." She got up and went to the kitchen. Paul heard the refrigerator door open, a clinking sound, then close. She came back with three bottles of Molson Golden in her hands and handed one each to Paul and Rick. "That's the only kind of beer you had," she said, looking at Rick. "You seriously need to up your game."

She twisted the top off her beer as the others did the same. Raising the bottle, she said, "To the numbered corporation, currently known as The Interstellar Company."

"To the Interstellar Company," Paul and Rick echoed. "*Salut!*"

That had been a week ago, and now it seemed that Rick had a contact on the fifty-meter telescope team. Paul hoped they'd found something.

Chapter 2: The Green Spot

Kingston, Ontario

Rick McDonald read through the file of astronomical data his contact had sent him. The person who Dr. Kercheval had mentioned to him, Tim Hawes, had been friendly enough and, like Rick, a fan of classic science fiction. That had proven useful, and their email exchanges had become discussions about topics ranging from the differences between actual nearby stars and planets as compared to those as described by authors like Gordon Dickson or Alastair Reynolds, to completely hypothetical arguments over which was the home star of Larry Niven's alien species the Kdatlyno (their conclusion, probably Gliese 884, 26.6 light-years from Sol, and, as a K-type star, on the target list for the fifty-meter telescope . . . sometime next year).

Out of those discussions, Hawes had sent Rick the raw observational data on those stars, with the understanding that he wouldn't publish anything based on that data.

Rick remembered this while wading through the numbers, and shook his head. *No fear of that.* While Rick had an interest in astronomy and the related physics, he was more of a hands-on guy. He liked building things, or figuring out the practical aspects of what the data described, not the teasing out of clues hidden in the third decimal place of a series of numbers. Sure, he could *do* the latter, but it wasn't *fun.*

On the positive side, it looked like a lot of the nearby sun-like stars had promising planets. *This one, for example, 82 Eridani*, he thought, checking the data summary. A G-type star, it had been known for the last sixty years to have three "super-Earths"—planets bigger than Earth but smaller than Neptune—in close orbit, too close to be habitable, but their presence had masked the fainter signal of an Earth-sized planet orbiting in the habitable zone. On the negative side, most of those same stars were out of easy reach of current starships. That same 82 Eridani was 19.8 light years from Sol, and almost 19.2 light years from Alpha Centauri. No ship had that kind of range. One of the newest models, with a twelve-light-year range, might do it, by way of Tau Ceti, if there were somewhere to refuel in that system.

Tau Ceti itself was a possible candidate, but the planet in its habitable zone was probably too large, massing nearly four times Earth. Rick didn't think that even the latest starships had the thrust needed to lift from a planet with the kind of gravity that implied. *No doubt about it*, he thought, *humanity needs to up its game.* That was one reason he'd gone into engineering physics. He hoped one day to parlay that into a career building better starships. Current technology still had nothing on *Star Trek.*

He moved on to the next star on his list, Delta Pavonis. It too looked promising, but at 19.9 light years, it was a tenth of a light year even farther than 82 Eridani. Maybe he could find a route to it with steps shorter than his limit, if the planet looked any good.

∞ ∞ ∞

Paul Fabron looked up from his reader as Rick came bounding down the stairs from his room. "What's up?"

"I've found a destination for us," Rick announced, somewhat breathlessly.

"Whoa, slow down. What are you talking about?"

"A little while ago I got an email from my contact on the fifty-meter telescope team. I looked at their preliminary data and found a candidate planet for us. It looks a little odd, but it's in the habitable zone, with a strong oxygen line."

"Oh? What do you mean, odd?" Paul assumed that *oxygen line* meant something in the planet's spectrum.

"It's green. An Earthlike planet should look like a pale blue dot, dominated by oceans and clouds. All the others discovered so far do."

"All four of them, you mean? Earth, Kakuloa, Sawyer's World, and whatever they're calling the one orbiting Epsilon Eridani—"

"That's Spitzer. The Chinese never registered a name."

"*Peu importe*, whatever. Four isn't much of a sample size. Can we see any details?"

"No, just a couple of blurry pixels. But it's now a sample of five. They recently confirmed another at Epsilon Indi. Also, whatever's orbiting Tau Ceti is blue and has oxygen, although the mass estimate seems high for a terraformed planet. But the green here probably means that there's more land area, so more forests or grasslands."

"Or chlorine in the atmosphere, or something," Paul said skeptically.

"No, that would show in the spectrum."

"So where is this destination? You didn't mention the star."

"Delta Pavonis."

Paul recognized the name, although he couldn't recall the details. He raised his wrist and queried his omniphone.

"*Delta Pavonis is a southern hemisphere star in the constellation Pavo,*" it returned. "*It is a solitary, G-type star—*" a sun-like star was good "*—making it the nearest solar analog not part of a multiple star system—*" So why hadn't anyone visited it yet? "*—at a distance of 19.9 light years.*"

"Stop," he said. The omni shut up.

He looked at Rick. "Almost twenty light years? No wonder it hasn't been visited. There aren't any ships with that kind of range. And I thought Epsilon Indi and Tau Ceti were closer?"

"Yes they are, but they're K-type stars, slightly cooler than Sol, not G-type."

"Kakuloa's sun is K-type, isn't it? But still, Delta Pavonis is too far. That's not a destination."

"There are some long-range ships," Rick protested. "Granted, they are mostly fuel tank. But we can reach it with a standard-range ship. The longest leg is less than ten light years."

Paul looked at his friend intently. "Are you sure? Then why hasn't anyone gone there yet?"

"I'm sure. As for why, it might be because of the odd color, but mainly it's because the last step was only recently confirmed possible. We go via Epsilon Indi. From there, it is only 9.2 light years to Delta Pavonis. As I mentioned earlier, confirmation that Epsilon Indi III is terraformed is new. They call it Taprobane."

That meant they'd have to refuel on a newly-discovered terraformed planet. *Bien*, that would be good practice for the landing he wanted to do on a brand-new planet. But with this new route opened up, there would likely be others who realized that Delta Pavonis was now within reach, green-colored planet or not.

"How far is it to, how did you call it, Taprobane?"

Rick hesitated before answering. "It's 11.8 light years, but—"

"That's more than ten, so too far. Why bring it up?"

"It's 11.8 light years from *here*. It's less than 9.7 light years from Alpha Centauri. We just make one more stop."

Paul thought it over. More than four light years to Alpha Centauri, another ten to Epsilon Indi, and then just over nine to Delta Pavonis. Roughly twenty-four light years, each way, plus time to maneuver and refuel. That would be a two-month round trip, not counting however long they stayed to explore the new planet, if it was indeed terraformed. If it wasn't . . . but Rick had said it showed a strong oxygen line. That and the green *had* to mean photosynthetic life of some kind. If it wasn't terraformed, that in itself would be a significant discovery. It might not be as valuable a find if humans couldn't live there, but on the other hand, who knew what biochemicals such an ecosystem might harbor? The pharmaceutical companies had an intense interest in the Alpha Centauri system for just that reason. The more he thought about it, the better it sounded.

"Rick, *mon ami*, I think you have indeed found our destination, and our company name, the Delta Pavonis Company. No, wait, that's too obvious. Maybe the Pavonis Company? Isn't there a mountain of that name on Mars?"

"Yes, Pavonis Mons, an extinct volcano. Or you could call it the Peacock Company, Pavonis is Latin for peacock. *Paon* in French, I think."

"I like that. Paon Company," Paul said. "Now all we need is a ship. I need to make some calls."

Chapter 3: Old Explorers

Franklin Drake's office, the Pentagon

"Commodore Drake, there's a call from a Mr. Fabron for you."

"Fabron? Yes, put him through." Drake of course knew Fabron Industries; they had been a subcontractor on the V-class ships. Perhaps they wanted in on his new project.

Keying his desk phone, Drake said, "*Bonjour Monsieur* Fabron, what can I do for you?"

There was a moment of silence, then a voice Drake did not recognize, but with a slight French accent, said, "I'm sorry, Commodore Drake, there may have been some misunderstanding. This is *Paul* Fabron, not my father Pierre, calling. To be honest, my business doesn't directly involve my father's company at all."

"Oh? Well, no matter." In fact, Drake was a little irked, but more at his assistant's mishandling than at Fabron *fils*. "What can I do for you?"

"I am putting together a private deep space exploration venture, and for various reasons, I don't want to rely solely on my father's connections. I'm wondering if I could interest you in a position on the board of directors? It would take very little of your time, and of course, you would be compensated."

Drake understood immediately; this wasn't the first such offer he had had, although none had been from anyone with Paul Fabron's connections. "Let me see if I understand. You want to establish yourself independently of your father—which I commend, by the way—but you'd also like some well-known names on your board for the recognition. I take it this would be largely a figurehead position?"

"Uh, I congratulate you on your insight, sir. As to the position, it could be as hands-on as you wish, but bear in mind that salary would mostly be in stock shares at this point. Still, if you want to pilot a starship. . . ."

The last caught Drake by surprise. He never expected to fly a starship again, despite his triumphant return after rescuing the crew of the *Anderson*, although in truth, he had been responsible for leaving them behind at Alpha Centauri in the first place. "This is an interstellar voyage? You have a ship?"

"*Oui*, and not yet. We're still working on that. I had hoped you might be able to help there."

"Huh." Drake had plenty to keep him busy here. He was overseeing the development of an upgraded class of starship, one with much greater range than the Vanguard class, let alone the old *Heinlein* and *Anderson* ships. It sounded like young Fabron's company was more daydream than actuality. "I'm not sure I can help. Who else do you have on your board?"

"To be honest, you're the first person I've contacted. I have a meeting set up with Dr. George Darwin, and—"

"George? Well, give him my regards." Drake knew George Darwin, the exobiologist, very well. They had been together on the expedition that had first discovered life on Mars, then again on the first mission to Alpha Centauri. In fact, Darwin had made the first footsteps on an extrasolar planet. He could see why Paul would want to get Darwin on board. But then, so did everybody else. "Look, *Monsieur* Fabron," Drake continued, "let me be blunt. You're not the first to approach me to be on the board of some space-related venture, and I doubt you'll be the last, and I'm sure the same goes for George Darwin, or anyone else from the first expedition. I wish you good luck, and some of them may even be interested, but I am still Space Force, so any such position would likely be a conflict of interest. I'm afraid I must decline."

"Ah, well, thank you for your time, sir." Drake could hear the disappointment in Paul's voice. He sympathized, remembering his own efforts to get out from under his father's influence. Heck, that was why he'd joined the military in the first place. Maybe he could do something for the young man.

"There is one thing," he said.

"*Oui*?"

"You said you needed a ship. It's a long shot, and it may not suit your needs, but there is one ship I'm aware of that was intended for interstellar flight, but currently not in use."

"Oh? Please go on."

The ship Drake was thinking of should have accompanied the first Alpha Centauri expedition, but it had been withdrawn for repairs. Those made, China had then repossessed its borrowed fusion reactor for their own use. "You'll need to replace the fusion system, and I don't know what else, but last I heard, the *Jules Verne* is sitting in a hangar at the Kourou Space Port. You might follow up on that. You could probably get a good deal."

"The *Jules Verne*?" Drake could almost hear the gears turning in young Fabron's head. "That would take some work, but . . . I like it! Thank you, sir."

"Not at all. And again, good luck. *Bonne chance!*" *You'll need it*, Drake added, silently, as he clicked off.

∞ ∞ ∞

Kingston, Ontario

"Okay," Paul said to the others after the call, "Drake is not interested in joining our company, and I understand his reasons. He did give me a lead on a possible ship, though."

"Really?" Rick said. "What ship?"

"I'll tell you when I have more information. It's only a lead. My next step is to meet with Dr. George Darwin, at Cornell."

"In Ithaca?" Mary said. Ithaca, New York, was a three-hour drive from Kingston.

"*Oui*. Is there another Cornell?"

"Do you want me to fly you down? It's two-hundred kilometers straight south of here. We'll have to rent a plane, of course."

"Can I come?" Rick said eagerly.

The offer surprised Paul, but it made sense, and would save him several hours. He nodded. "*D'accord, bien sûr*. But Rick, you'll have to sit in the back."

"Story of my life," he said, grinning.

∞ ∞ ∞

Dr. George Darwin's office, Cornell U.

George Darwin looked up at the young man who'd just entered his office. Paul Fabron didn't look any older than most of his students, but he was dressed in a business suit.

"Thank you for seeing me, Doctor Darwin," he said. "It's an honor to meet you."

"Thanks, but don't go all fan-boy on me, Mr. Fabron. I've had enough of that. Call me George."

"And I'm Paul. I'll get to the point. I'm looking to mount an expedition to Delta Pavonis, and I'd like your support. Even to come along, if you're willing."

Darwin eyed him skeptically. The man—boy—couldn't have been more than twenty-four at most. But his family did have a lot of money. "You're mounting the expedition? Personally, or is this something your father's company is behind?"

Paul reddened slightly. "My father is not involved. This is an independent venture. PaonCo has been incorporated to carry it out."

"Ponco?" Darwin echoed, puzzled.

"Paon Company. Paon is French for peacock."

"Ah," Darwin said, understanding. "Peacock, pavonis. So, what does Delta Pavonis have going for it, and why would I be interested?"

"It's a sun-like star a bit less than twenty light years from here. It has an Earth-mass planet in its habitable zone—"

"So, another terraformed planet," Darwin interrupted. "Been there, done that, named the planet, almost lost crew members. So have several other people. We're up to at least four the last I heard. If you want to put your name on one, good for you, but again, why would I be interested?"

"For one thing, it's green."

"What?" That did catch his interest. Terraformed planets looked blue-white from space, or at least, all the ones found so far did. You wouldn't get vegetation covering an arid planet; you had to have oceans. "Green, you say?"

Paul nodded. "*Oui.* The fifty-meter telescope shows a green planet, not the blue and white marble of Earthlike planets. There's something different about it."

Paul had Darwin's attention now. One of his disappointments with Kakuloa—and Sawyer's World, although he hadn't set foot on that one—was that the life had clearly descended from terrestrial forms imported tens of millions of years earlier. As an exobiologist, he had been searching for different life, something with a truly alien biochemistry. The question of whether what he'd found on Mars had evolved there or on Earth first was unanswerable; they both had the same biochemistry. But, green?

"That's more likely to be something in the atmosphere," Darwin said. "Chlorine, perhaps." That would be unlikely, and as exciting as finding free oxygen. Elemental chlorine would react with rocks in a geological instant. It would take an active process—like life—to maintain it in an atmosphere. But it was far scarcer than oxygen.

"No," Paul said. "That's what I said at first, but the spectrograms don't show chlorine. They *do* show free oxygen. There's life there, but perhaps not as we know it."

Darwin scoffed at that last. "I can imagine a few ways that life as we do know it could make a planet look green. Maybe the oceans are shallow, and it's all swamp. I assume there's water vapor in the atmosphere?"

"Yes, of course."

"Well, there you go then. But you knew all that before you came to me. What is it you actually want, my name recognition? You've got your own."

Paul nodded. "I do, but of course, adding yours would help build up more backing. But your experience is really what I was looking for. We need an experienced exobiologist, and—"

"If it's terraformed, which I suspect it is—an Earth-mass planet in the habitable zone of a sun-like star? Have you figured out the day length yet? I'll bet it's within ten percent of twenty-four hours."

Paul shrugged. "The light curve is irregular. It might be, but it's hard to say at this distance. The color may be in the atmosphere, but it's masking the rotation."

"Huh." That was curious. An Earth-sized planet would be too big for a planetary dust storm like Mars sometimes experienced. Something like dust but green in the atmosphere? Algae? The puzzle was almost enough to make Darwin want to go and see for himself. Almost, but not quite. "Well, that doesn't prove it's not. As I was saying, if it *is* terraformed, you don't need an exobiologist; a biologist would do."

"That's not your only qualification," Paul said. "You also have experience on *Anderson* class starships."

"I've flown on them, of course, but I'm not a pilot. Anyway, you're not going in anything like that; there aren't any." The *USS Poul Anderson* itself, and the Russian *Krechet*, had been left in the Alpha Centauri system. The *Chandrasekhar* was a historical monument, still parked near the quarantine base on the Moon, and the *Heinlein*, while not technically *Anderson* class, was also a historical ship that wouldn't be going anywhere but for training flights within the solar system. And while those ships had been built from modified commercial SSTO rockets, the technology was now obsolete, and there had never been the Chinese-built fusion reactors available to adapt more. That's why the return mission to Alpha Centauri had taken so long.

"Actually, there is one," Paul said with a slight smile.

"What are you talk— Wait, you don't mean . . ." Darwin's voice trailed off at Paul's widening grin.

"Yes, the *Jules Verne.* My intention is to refit it with modern fusors."

"Now I know you're crazy. Are you going to make this a one-ship expedition? What if something goes wrong?"

"Is that what you said to the crew of the *Anderson* before they chose to land on planet Able?"

Darwin flushed, his temper rising. At least this young pup hadn't called it Sawyer's World. Saying goodbye to Elizabeth Sawyer before she took the *Anderson* down had been one of the hardest things he had ever done, and he had fully expected never to see her again. In fact, for the most part, he had not. He had declined Frank Drake's invitation to go along on the *Endeavour* for the rescue mission, afraid that all they would find would be dead bodies. He had encountered her once, when she had returned to Earth briefly, and it had been awkward.

"What I said to them is none of your business," Darwin finally choked out, "and they are *damned* lucky to have survived. There's a reason that planet is named what it is." Sawyer herself had protested the name, but the rest of her crew had insisted.

Paul was instantly apologetic. "*Je m'excuse*, I'm sorry, I meant no offense. You are right. Going in a single ship *is* dangerous. But now there are many other ships that can make the trip. We will arrange for follow-up if we don't return in a timely manner."

Darwin allowed himself to be mollified. It wasn't as though he hadn't done his share of risky things when he was Paul Fabron's age.

"What about the rest of your crew? Do they understand the risks?"

"I won't take anyone who doesn't."

Darwin had his doubts, and his skepticism must have shown.

"If you want," Paul said, "you can ask them yourself. Two of them are here; they flew down with me from Kingston."

Darwin let it pass. But there was another problem. "Twenty light years, you said? The *Jules Verne* won't get you more than five."

"The upgrades will give us at least a ten light-year range. We'll do it in multiple hops, refueling at each stop."

"What's your route?"

"First to Alpha Centauri, then to Epsilon Indi, and from there to Delta Pavonis. Each step is less than ten light years."

Darwin nodded slowly. If Paul was right about the range, that could work. But the stop at Alpha Centauri, even if it were Kakuloa and not Sawyer's World, was another reason he wanted no part of the trip. Still, Delta Pavonis, and a green planet?

"That much you seem to have thought out," he told Paul.

"I've studied all the expedition reports, especially those from your mission," the young man responded. "We intend to bring a geologist and an exobiologist, or at least a biologist. We already have a pilot and an engineer/astrophysicist."

"Hmm." Darwin found himself mulling it over. A green planet? Even if it were just some odd configuration of Earth-descended life, it might be interesting, and getting out in the field again . . . No. He had to admit it to himself, field biology in an unknown environment was a younger man's game. "It sounds fascinating," he said, meaning it. "If I were ten years younger, I might take you up on it, but I'm getting way too old for this shit."

"But it was only eight years ago that you went to Alpha Centauri."

"And I'm not sorry, but in hindsight— Never mind, enough about that."

"Is there perhaps someone you would recommend?"

Darwin thought about it. There were a couple of former students and others he'd worked with who might be interested, but he wouldn't mention them to young Fabron until he was more comfortable that the mission wouldn't end in catastrophe. Elizabeth and her team had managed to survive, barely, but he'd lived for four years with the fear and near certainty that they hadn't. He didn't want to go through that again.

"I might have a couple of names. Let me give it some thought, and see how they feel."

"Very well. I would ask again, please don't disclose our planned destination. Right now, I think Delta Pavonis is not seen as a likely target; I'd like to keep it that way."

"You want to be first."

"Of course. Not only for me, but for *Jules Verne*."

Darwin had to grin at that. If it had just been for Paul, he might have discounted it, but the *Verne* should have been part of the Centauri mission. Darwin could sympathize with that request. "Of course," he said.

"Thank you for your time," Paul said, rising to leave. "Oh, one other thing."

"Yes?"

"I'd like to set up a meeting with Centauri Pharmaceuticals to discuss backing for the expedition, you understand?"

Darwin did. The biology of any new world could lead to valuable new drugs. It was just such that had helped finance the return mission to Alpha Centauri in the first place. "Would you like an introduction?"

"That's more than I was going to ask. I just wondered if I might mention your name."

"I'll do better than that. Hold on a moment."

Darwin's omniphone was on his wrist. He tapped it and said, "Victoria Holmes, Skrellan Pharmaceuticals." He grinned as he saw Paul's eyes widen.

Victoria Holmes's personal receptionist answered, and to her query he said, "This is George Darwin. Please tell Victoria that a young man named Paul Fabron will be contacting her, or I guess you, to set up a meeting to discuss a business proposition, and that I thought she'd be interested."

He paused as the receptionist repeated that back to him.

"Yes," he continued, "Paul Fabron. F-A-B-R-O-N. Yes, *exactly* like the billionaire. Thanks. Have her give me a call back whenever it's convenient. Thank you." He tapped off.

Paul was still standing there, but he'd recovered his composure. Darwin imagined that given who his father was, calls like this wouldn't be too far out of his experience. "Will that do, Paul?"

"Thank you, Doctor Dar— er, George. That was very generous. But, while you have your omni, could I get her number?"

Darwin chuckled. That *would* be easier than going through the main switchboard. He tapped his phone to send the number to Paul's.

"I ask one favor in return," Darwin added.

"Of course, what?"

"If you *do* find non-terrestrial life there, I want to be the first to know when you get back. Actually, contact me when you get back regardless."

Paul nodded. "*Bien sûr*," he said. "Of course. I wouldn't have it any other way."

∞ ∞ ∞

"Well?" Rick was the first to ask when Paul met up with them again.

"He won't be joining us," Paul said. "Frankly, I would have surprised if he wanted to, especially on such short notice. But he will give some thought to recommending a biologist to us."

"Is that all?" Mary said, her shoulders slumped. "This isn't going to work, is it?"

"*Mais non*," Paul said. "He also arranged for me to meet with Victoria Holmes to discuss business arrangements."

"Who?" she asked.

Paul thought everyone knew the story. "She helped form the partnership that is Centauri Pharmaceuticals and arranged the financing to expedite the return expedition to Alpha Centauri. They even named one of the ships after her."

"*Actually*," Rick said, drawling out the word, "they named *Victoria* for Magellan's ship, the first to circumnavigate the Earth."

Paul and Mary both looked at him and grinned. "That," Paul said, "is just the *official* reason. The one they want you to believe."

Chapter 4: Drug Money

Skrellan Pharmaceuticals, Earth

"Thank you for seeing me, Ms. Holmes," Paul Fabron said after being ushered into her office.

"Please, call me Victoria," she said. "George Darwin said you had something to discuss that could be worth my time. He was cagey on the details, but I trust him enough to give you a few minutes." *But this had better be good*, she thought. "So, what can I do for you?"

"All right, I'll get to the point. My start-up, PaonCo, would like Centauri Pharmaceuticals' backing for an expedition to what we believe is a new terraformed planet. In exchange, we'll give you exclusive license to anything of biopharmaceutical interest that we find. Something similar to your arrangement on Kakuloa."

Victoria was a seasoned enough negotiator to not blink. Given the Fabron connection, she had expected something beyond Darwin hoping for a job for one of his grad students, and young Paul hadn't disappointed. She hadn't quite expected *this*, though. "Well, you're not asking for much, are you?" she said. "Do you know how much we spent on Kakuloa?"

"As a matter of fact, I do," he said, naming the figure. "I also know that most of that went to ship construction and development, much of which you also retained rights to. That won't be needed in our case; we have a ship."

"All right, you have my attention. But two things first."

"Yes?"

"One, you said, quote, 'my start-up,' not 'our start-up.' Do I take it then that, um, none of your family members are involved?"

"You mean my father."

"Well, yes. I apologize for the question; I'm just making sure I understand."

"*Bien sûr,* of course. No, my father is not involved, nor is anyone else at Fabron Industries. To be honest, I would rather raise the necessary funding without touching any of his, if possible. I do have other associates, of course. And the other thing?"

"Fair enough, we can go into that in more detail if we end up working together. Which does bring me to my second point.

"I work for *Skrellan* Pharmaceuticals," she continued, emphasizing the name. "Granted, we're the largest partner in Centauri Pharmaceuticals, but we're not Centauri. Did you specifically want to deal with Centauri, or would an exclusive with Skrellan work? That is, assuming we could afford it."

Victoria thought she detected a slight smile on Paul's face. Whatever his relationship might be with his father, she had no doubt that he'd learned a lot from him.

"It might well simplify things to work directly and exclusively with Skrellan. We can certainly make that assumption going forward unless and until Skrellan decides it wants to share the risk."

"And just how much risk are we talking about? Where is this new terraformed planet, and what makes you think you'd be able to offer us an exclusive? That means you have to be first to land on it and bring back useful data."

"*Oui*, of course. The usual non-disclosure agreements?"

"Naturally."

They both brought out their omnis. Paul sent hers the NDA he had already prepared. She glanced at it, then her contract-analysis app read it and made a couple of minor tweaks. The app couldn't handle anything significant, of course, but a simple non-disclosure agreement was easily within its capability. She thumb-printed the revised copy and sent it back to Paul.

"Is that satisfactory?" she asked.

He glanced at it, tapped his omni, probably running similar software on it, then thumb-printed it and returned it. "Perfectly, thank you."

"So, where and why?"

"A sun-like star, G-type, called Delta Pavonis. It's under twenty light years from here, and sixteen-and-a-half from Alpha Centauri. Less than ten from Epsilon Indi."

"So, on the edge of explored space, but not too far out. I haven't heard of any planet there, but what makes you think you'll be first?"

"Two reasons. There are closer candidates, both to here and to Alpha Centauri. For example, 70 Ophiuchi and 61 Cygni. Now, they're both double stars, but so is Alpha Centauri." Paul had obviously done his homework. So far he hadn't referred to any notes.

"Do they have planets?"

"It's harder to tell with doubles," he said. "There have been numerous unconfirmed reports for both, and they're on the list for observation with the fifty-meter space telescope. But we're not interested in those. Let somebody else go look first, if they're not already on their way."

"So why Delta Pavonis?"

"It *does* have a planet orbiting in the habitable zone. Normally that would be tempting enough for someone to go look, at least."

"You said, 'normally.' Why haven't they?"

"Mostly, because nobody knows it's there, not yet. How much detail do you want?"

"Keep going. I'll tell you when to stop." She understood the basics, and she was curious as to Paul Fabron's grasp of them.

She'd known too many eager entrepreneurs who could talk a good sales game but were clueless when it came to technical details.

Paul shrugged. "*D'accord.* The astronomers know Delta Pavonis has planets, but they're not well characterized. The system is at the wrong angle to ours, so the planets' effect on the star is less. It has a known Jovian in a twelve-year orbit. It masks fainter signals from smaller planets, but they've teased out a bit."

"So, you're basing this trip on what, a hint of a wobble within a wobble of a star's position?" She had made it a point to study up on exoplanets, and how they were detected, back at the time of the second Alpha Centauri expedition, just in case other opportunities—like the one Paul Fabron offered—came up.

"Oh, more than that. The fifty-meter space telescope has imaged it, but the paper hasn't been published yet. One of my associates knows somebody."

This sounded more promising by the minute, but Paul's hint of a looming deadline made her cautious. That was a typical salesman's pressure tactic. She eyed him skeptically. "If it looked terraformed, there would have been a preliminary announcement, surely?"

Paul was unfazed. "*Oui*, only *if* it looked terraformed. This one doesn't. It's green. Until they rule out all other explanations, they're not going to say anything, for fear of, what's the expression? Eggs on their face."

"Have *you* ruled out other explanations?"

"A lot of them, yes. Its spectrum shows a very strong oxygen line, also other lines consistent with a roughly Earth-like atmosphere."

She began to understand Darwin's interest. "Then why is it green?"

"We'll know when we get there. George Darwin suggested it might be a planet-wide swamp; we'd still expect some white from clouds, but the resolution of the telescope image is only a few pixels. It would blur together."

Victoria sat back, thinking. Any vegetation, even pond scum, with sixty-some million years of evolution independent of Earth, could have come up with biochemicals never seen before on any other planet. Computer modeling could generate new compounds, but that search space might as well be infinite. In real life, millions of years of natural selection narrowed it down to what was biochemically interesting. What Centauri Pharmaceuticals had found on Kakuloa and Sawyer's World was evidence enough of that. Some of those were already beginning to pay off, and others would make fortunes when they were approved for distribution. The anti-aging compound in squidberry extract alone would be worth several times what that mission had cost.

And if there were nothing there? If the planet was green for some non-organic reason? That was unlikely, with oxygen in the atmosphere, but who knew what surprises space held? As Director of Research, Victoria well knew how much money Skrellan spent on projects that never panned out. This one might well be worth the risk, but she—and Paul's company—would have to act on it quickly before the information leaked out and someone else got the same idea.

"All right, Paul, let's talk details. Just how much do you need?"

Chapter 5: Jules Verne

Kingston, Ontario

After returning from his meeting with Victoria Holmes, Paul made another call to the agent he had engaged to follow up on the lead Commodore Drake had given him. Then he spent the better part of a day in multiple calls to Skrellan Pharmaceuticals, his bank, their bank, the Kourou Spaceport, his agent again, and more. Finally, he staggered into the living room, interrupting some irrelevant discussion between Mary and Rick.

"It is official," he announced. "The Paon Company is now the proud owner of the starship *Jules Verne*, contingent on our inspection."

"All right!" Rick said. "When?"

"Is that the name we're going with?" Mary asked.

"What do you mean? That is its name," Paul said, puzzled.

"As the new owners," she said, "we can name it anything we like. That's simply a matter of filing the forms. We have to change the numbers anyway, don't we?"

"The registration number, yes," he said. "Of course, it keeps the original serial numbers. But the name?"

"I was thinking perhaps *Galileo*," Mary said.

"What? Why? He was Italian."

Rick grinned but said nothing. He must know something Paul didn't.

"No, I meant in reference to *Rocketship Ga—*" Mary started, then broke off. "Never mind."

Paul considered. "You know, when the ship was first commissioned, and the US ships were already going to be named after classic American science fiction writers who had also had military service—"

"Yeah," Rick interrupted. "The next in the series would have been the *Jerry Pournelle.*"

Paul frowned at him. "As I was saying," he resumed, "there was an active campaign in Europe to name the ship after a science-fictional military space hero . . . Perry Rhodan."

"Who?" Mary asked.

Paul sighed. "I suppose he wasn't as big over here. In Europe, he was huge, with thousands of novels and stories published. As big as Star Trek or Star Wars for a while, although not nearly so much now as back then. A lot of it is very dated. I was a fan briefly, as a kid. In fact, I supported the naming campaign."

Rick had been listening. He would know the reference. "So, you want to rename it the *Perry Rhodan*?"

Paul chuckled. "Hah. Now that you've brought it up, I am tempted to. It's just the kind of joke that would piss a lot of people off, my father especially." He shook his head. "*Mais non.* I don't think that would help our fund-raising efforts at all. Besides, now I like the name *Jules Verne.* French science fiction writers deserve recognition too."

"And there's the real reason," Mary said wryly, "that notorious Gallic pride."

Paul looked at her and smiled. It was a running joke. "Notorious? I think you meant, *understandable.*"

"Whatever," Rick said. "The *Jules Verne* it is. But when do we get to see the ship?"

Mary asked, "And how do I get checked out on it?"

∞ ∞ ∞

"First things first," Paul said. "What's the status of your spacecraft certification?" He knew she had taken the test on the relevant spaceflight regulations a few days earlier, and he believed her when she told him that she was sure she had aced it, but the results had to be officially approved.

"Good question," she said. "I got the notification that I had passed, but last time I looked, my certificate hadn't been upgraded. Let me check." She tapped a sequence on her omniphone, scrolled down the screen a bit, then yelped "Got it!" She held up her omni so the others could see the screen and looked at them, beaming.

The image showed her pilot's license, with the endorsement "Approved for spaceflight operations" added to it, with a section marked "Ratings." The space beside that was marked "N/A."

"What does that mean?" Rick asked her.

"It means I have to be checked out on specific spacecraft types to be allowed to fly them. It's not like a simple aircraft license where you're allowed to fly, say, anything massing less than two thousand kilos. Bigger aircraft, or spacecraft, have more specialized systems. It's mostly a holdover from old pre-space days, when everything wasn't quite so automated. The spaceflight endorsement means they're happy that I understand the regulations, astronavigation, life support, and so on. The type rating, for a given type of vehicle, means I know which buttons to push and where they're located.

"Bringing me back to my original question, Paul. How do I get checked out on the *Jules Verne*?"

"I'm working on that. We need to go take possession, and then spend a week or two getting the ship ready for space while the manufacturer trains us on its systems."

"Us?"

"I want everyone to have basic knowledge of the ship, although Mary will be the pilot. I'm going to take a cram course to get my spacecraft rating."

"You won't have the flight hours," Mary objected.

"I know, but other than that, I'll have the paper qualifications. It will help me understand what I'm asking you to do."

"Fine with me. Just so long as my word goes when we're in flight, even if you are the boss."

"Of course." He glanced over at Rick. "What about you? Want to learn how to fly a spaceship?"

"Only in theory," he said. "Sure, I want to know how it works, and what not to do, but I'm happy to leave the details to someone else, eh? Like, I'm fine with autocabs, so I don't see the need for a driver's license. But sure, I'll take the training on the systems. Where, by the way? You never mentioned where the *Jules Verne* is now."

"You're right. Are you up for a little trip? If your passports aren't in order, you need to get that fixed."

"Shouldn't be a problem. Where are we headed?"

"Kourou Spaceport, French Guiana. Pack for warm weather."

Chapter 6: Rivals

Baylor Chemical Industries, Earth

Edward Talbot wondered why he'd been summoned to Jay Noske's office at Baylor Chemical. As lead pilot at Zodiac Starlines, Talbot commanded the starship *Matthew*, chartered for regular cargo runs to the Alpha Centauri system. Zodiac was actually an arms-length subsidiary of Baylor Chemical Industries, one of the members of the Centauri Pharmaceuticals partnership. Baylor liked to keep fingers in lots of pies, but Talbot didn't understand why anyone there would need to talk to *him*. In any case, the *Matthew* was due to stand down for at least a month for maintenance and upgrades. Given Mr. Noske's title, Director for Special Projects, Talbot presumed there was some special project Noske had in mind.

"Captain Talbot, thanks for coming," Noske said as Talbot was shown into the office.

Talbot shook the extended hand, saying, "Just 'Edward' or 'Ed' is fine, Mr. Noske, when I'm not aboard ship. What did you want to see me about?"

"Well Ed—and call me Jay, by the way—something interesting has come up. But first, can we offer you refreshment? Coffee, water?"

"No, I'm fine thanks," Talbot said, as he seated himself in the offered chair.

Noske nodded briskly and then, to his aide, said, "That will be all, thank you. Close the door on your way out." He waited until the two of them were alone in the room, then, in a more serious tone, said, "I understand your ship is off the regular cargo run for a while."

"It is, yes. What's this about? I'm guessing it has something to do with a special project?"

"It does indeed. You understand this conversation is not to be discussed? It falls under the terms of the non-disclosure agreements between you, Zodiac, and Baylor."

"Of course. Does it involve my ship, the *Matthew*?"

"It might. That's still to be determined, but is it ready for space? There was something about maintenance."

"It needs some minor routine maintenance, and we were planning to take advantage of the slack in the schedule for some major upgrades, but those can be postponed if necessary. Why?"

Noske didn't answer immediately. Instead, he kept looking at the display screen on his desk. It was angled so Talbot couldn't see it. After a moment, Noske said, "What do you know about Delta Pavonis?"

Interesting question, Talbot thought. He tried to recall what he did know. "It's a nearby star, sun-like, roughly twenty light years from here. Out of range for a trip from Sol, and I'd have to look at a chart to see if it can be reached from, say, Alpha Centauri. It's a southern hemisphere star, so it might be, but as far as I know, nobody has been there. Again, why?"

"Does it have a terraformed planet?"

"I haven't heard of one. We know it has at least one planet, Jupiter-sized, but I don't remember hearing anything to suggest there are others that might be terraformed. But like I said, nobody has been there, so who knows? Is that what this is about? You want me to go look? That's a bit of a long shot, isn't it?"

"It does have a planet of the right mass and orbit to be Earthlike, though, does it not?"

"Again, I'd have to review the available data. But that doesn't mean it's terraformed; it could be uninhabitable. From what I recall, there are no blue planets in the system."

"No, there aren't," Noske said with a half-smile. "But there *is* a green one in the right place, and it shows a strong oxygen line in its spectrum."

This was news to Talbot. "Where did you hear this?"

"I was alerted to an as yet unpublished paper on just such an observation from the fifty-meter telescope. I've heard possible corroboration from other sources, but we can go into that later."

Talbot didn't bother to ask how Noske got his hands on an "as yet unpublished paper," but it explained why he hadn't heard of it yet himself. And he began to see Noske's interest.

"You want someone to go out there to check, and if there is anything biochemically interesting, terraformed or not, stake a claim on it." Talbot was up for that kind of mission. It beat routine freight runs back and forth to Kakuloa. It wouldn't be without risk, but that was fine with him.

Noske nodded. "Very close. There may be one catch, though."

"Oh?"

"We have reason to think that somebody else is already planning to 'go out there to check,' as you put it. Someone not engaged by Baylor or even Centauri Pharmaceuticals, but one of the other partners operating independently."

As independently as you apparently plan for Baylor to do, via me and the Matthew, Talbot surmised. "So, there's some urgency. What can you tell me about the competition?"

"Not a lot. I'm still collecting data. But there aren't many ships available for a trip like that on short notice—"

"None, I'd say. That's at least a month round trip, plus exploration time. I think I would have heard something. Unless it's a Space Force ship, but hasty voyages of exploration aren't really their style."

"Quite. Still, there's potentially a lot of money involved, and that has a way of shaking things loose."

"There is that," Talbot said. "So, how do you want to proceed?"

"Make plans for the mission. Don't commit the *Matthew* to any long-term maintenance yet, keep it to anything that is urgently needed or can be done quickly. I'll be finding out more within the next few days and give you a go or no-go then. Bill any time or expenses in the meantime to us, of course."

"What about crew selection? I assume my regular flight crew, but we'll want a science team for exploration, right?"

"Right. Leave that to me. I'll also arrange for any supplies that team will need. I just need you to ferry them there and back, assuming it's a go."

Talbot was a little leery of that aspect, but they'd taken occasional passengers on the *Matthew* before. Just so long as everyone understood who was ultimately in charge of the mission, but he didn't see any point in raising that right now.

"All right then," he said. "If that's all, I guess I have some maintenance to reschedule."

Chapter 7: Jungle

Cayenne, Capitol of French Guiana

The three of them—Paul, Mary, and Rick—walked out of the Cayenne - Félix Eboué Airport terminal and into the sweltering humidity of French Guiana.

"Ugh," Mary groaned, "is the weather always like this?"

"Pretty much, yes," Paul said, "We're only five hundred kilometers north of the equator, so it is like this, unless it's raining."

"Where to now?" Rick asked.

"Now we grab a cab to take us to Kourou. It's an hour's drive. I've arranged a place to stay in Kourou while we inspect the *Verne*."

Since its last return from space, the *Jules Verne* had been stored in an environmentally controlled hangar at the *Centre Spatial Guyanais*, or Guiana Space Centre. It had originally been assumed that *Jules Verne* would be returning to space shortly after some minor repairs and maintenance, so it made sense to keep it near the primary launch site for old vertical take-off chemical rockets, as opposed to returning it to the factory.

Paul Fabron had made a few trips to Kourou as a boy. He had accompanied his father on several of his many trips to the spaceport in the earlier days of his engineering business. The place was, if anything, even more hot and steamy than Paul remembered. He tried to recall the last time he'd been here. It was certainly before the *Verne* had even been built, and before that first robotic warp probe to Alpha Centauri. He'd been, what, ten or eleven? There had been a bodyguard with him back then, so yes, probably that age. He didn't really remember *why* he had a bodyguard, whether it was concern over criminal activity or political unrest, but as the son of someone rich and powerful, at least by local standards, he had been a potential kidnap target. There had also been something about occasional armed conflicts between illegal Brazilian gold miners and, if Paul remembered correctly, the *9e Régiment d'infanterie de marine*. That was farther south, near the border, not anywhere near Kourou. Here, the *3e Régiment étranger d'infanterie,* the Foreign Legion, was charged with security.

∞ ∞ ∞

As they drove north along highway N-1, dense forest limited the view beyond the road clearing. Only occasionally could they see buildings through the gaps cut by side-roads or driveways.

"Is it all like this?" Mary asked. "I had expected to see ocean. This kind of reminds me of some of the roads up north, except for the totally wrong kind of tree."

"*Oui*, pretty much," Paul said. "It's not a very densely settled country, especially when you get back more than ten kilometers or so from the coast. But we'll be crossing a bridge over the Cayenne River soon; you should get a better view then."

As he had said, a few minutes later the landscape opened up and the road crossed the low *Pont du Larivot*, with the wide muddy waters of the Cayenne River below them, and in the distance on their right, the Atlantic Ocean.

"This river is wider than I thought," Mary said. "Almost like the St. Lawrence. How long is this bridge?"

"I don't remember exactly. More than a kilometer. But this is the mouth of the river, and you're talking about the St. Lawrence at its source, where it drains Lake Ontario, right?"

"Yes, at Kingston. Point taken."

The trees surrounded them again as they left the bridge, although the scattered clearings occupied by houses or small businesses became more frequent. A few minutes farther on, they passed through the small town of Soula, and then some minutes after that, Tonate.

"Halfway there," Paul announced.

∞ ∞ ∞

A half-hour later they stood in the reception area of the Hotel Atlantis. It looked more like an upscale motel, with its spread out, two and three-story buildings, than a high-rise resort hotel. Kourou wasn't that kind of place, and the Atlantis, though aging, was still one of the better hotels in town.

Rick looked around the lobby, taking in the open architecture, the way the reception desk turned a corner to become the bar, and the open wall to the pool area. "You know, I'll have to admit I'd expected something a little more, I don't know, third-world? This place is actually pretty nice."

"We are in France, you know," Paul said, amused. "It may be a little corner of South America, but it is French territory. And there's a spaceport just three kilometers from here. Rocket scientists, and especially commercial customers, like their amenities, and this place was designed with them in mind."

"That actually makes sense."

"Anyway, let me get us checked in. Hand me your passports."

Documents in hand, Paul strode up to the reception desk where the clerk had been waiting for them.

"*Bonjour*," Paul said, "*je m'appelle Paul Fabron, vous avec une reservation pour la Compagnie Paon?*"

"*Bonjour, Monsieur Fabron.*" The conversation continued in French: "Welcome back to the Hotel Atlantis. It has been some years. Yes, we have been awaiting your arrival."

"You remember me? I'm sorry, I don't—"

The clerk smiled. "No, *monsieur*, our computers remember you. You stayed with your father, *n'est-ce pas*? I didn't even work here then."

"*Oui, bien sûr.*" Of course.

"Your rooms are all ready. Are you here for a launch? I wasn't aware of anything scheduled. We don't get many flights these days." They wouldn't. The old chemical rockets were fading like prop planes in the jet age.

"*Pas exactement*," Paul said, shaking his head. "We're here to take possession of the *Jules Verne* and to make sure that it's space-worthy."

"The *Jules Verne*? The starship? Excellent. Well, if there is anything we here at the Atlantis can do to make your stay more pleasant, please let us know."

"*Bien sûr*. I think right now we just want to check into our rooms and rest up after our trip."

"Certainly, sir." He glanced over at the others. They had all travelled light, with little more than a backpack each. "You're on the second floor," he said, handing over the room keys. "Shall I summon someone to help you with your bags?"

"No need," Paul said, "we're fine. *Merci beaucoup*." He took the keys and turned back to the others, reverting to English. "Upstairs," he gestured. "This way."

"My French must be rustier than I thought," Rick said. "I only caught about a third of that."

"The accent does take a bit of getting used to," Paul said, grinning, "but what you speak is Quebecois, not French."

Rick looked back at him, also smiling. "*Maudit français*," he muttered.

∞ ∞ ∞

Kourou Spaceport

Marcel Deschamps, a senior manager with Transpatiale, a European space transportation company, met the trio at the hotel after breakfast the next morning.

"Bonjour, *Monsieur* Fabron, and welcome to Kourou." Deschamps said as he greeted them. "I'll be escorting you onto the base today. After we get the security details taken care of, you will have access to both the *Jules Verne* and whatever facilities you need. Now, the details were unclear. You understand that because the *Verne* has been in storage for some time, it is naturally not immediately flight ready."

Paul nodded. "Of course. We were planning to make some changes anyway."

"I see. That is between you and your engineers. But in terms of pad interfacing, will you be providing your own launch prep team or . . . ?"

"I would like my people involved, of course, but I think it would be best to use a team that is familiar with how you do things here. It's my understanding that the *Verne* differs only a little from standard, from that point of view."

"Surely it doesn't need a pad?" Mary said. "After all, it was designed to land and take-off from a completely unprepared area at Alpha Centauri."

"You'll have to excuse Mary," Paul said before Deschamps could take offense. She is my chief pilot and has a lot of experience flying in the wilds of northern Canada."

"Ah, I see. You are correct, Ma'amselle," Deschamps said, "but at Alpha Centauri, there were no facilities and, to put it bluntly, nothing to be damaged if something unfortunate were to happen on launch. So, you were a . . . bush pilot? Is that the term?"

"Yes, and I was," Mary said, not quite sure where this was leading.

"Then you will be familiar with the concept. While in the bush, you may land and take off as you wish in accordance with the terrain, but if you are operating out of an airport, you conform to airport regulations, *n'est ce pas*?"

"Oh, of course. I understand. That makes perfect sense. Thank you." Mary wondered exactly how much "pad services" were going to add to the price tag, but didn't see any point in arguing the matter.

The drive to the spaceport, as locals referred to the Guiana Space Center, was a short one; the main gate was just a few kilometers up the road. Deschamps ushered the group through security and the process of getting badged, and then they were on their way to where the *Jules Verne* had been waiting to return to space.

∞ ∞ ∞

Hanger Seven, Kourou Spaceport

The outside of the hangar building gave Mary the impression of years of disuse. Like most other buildings in the humid tropical climate here, the white-painted walls were streaked with rust wherever steel fittings were attached, and green vegetation grew up around the base and clung in blotches like mold.

"I sure hope it looks better on the inside," she said as they approached the structure.

"Don't worry," Deschamps reassured them, "we keep the buildings well maintained. This is the tropics, and the plants are very aggressive. They grow back almost as quickly as they can be removed. There's no need to contaminate the area with weed killer, even if regulations allowed it."

"Not something you have to worry about back home, eh Mary?" Rick said.

"No, just bears and bugs."

"At least we have no bears here," Deschamps said, "but we do have jaguars and cougars. However, they mostly avoid human habitations." They had already discovered the bugs, or rather, the bugs—especially the mosquitoes—had discovered them.

The human-sized door set into the wall next to the main hangar door looked tiny by comparison. Deschamps waved them through. Inside, the lights were already on, and a technician waited to meet them.

After quick introductions, they donned coveralls, and then Mary immediately moved in for a walk-around, leaving Rick and Paul to talk with Deschamps and the technician.

The base of the ship was clad with black heat-shield tiles, all showing some streaking and discoloration from the *Verne*'s last flight. The lowest part of the base, at the center, was a meter off the floor. Mary ducked underneath the edge to get a closer look at it, and at the engines.

"Heat shield looks good," she called back. "I'll want to confirm that with the on-board diagnostics, of course."

She walked around beneath the ship to the gaps in the shield where the engines were mounted, a meter from the outer edge. The engine bells had red fabric covers over the openings. She peeled one away, then pulled a flashlight out of a coverall pocket and shone it up into the bell. As expected, it showed signs of use but no obvious corrosion or other damage. She raised her light to scan the injector plate. It too looked fine. There were also no animal or insect nests inside, one reason for the covers. "So far, so good," she called out, her voice echoing within the engine bell.

She ducked back out and made her way to the next engine opening. There was no nozzle. In fact, she saw, looking up into the cavity above her, where the propellant pipes were neatly capped off, there was no engine. *What the . . . ?*

"Hey, Paul, we're missing an engine!"

"What?"

Mary ducked under again and lay flat on the floor, scanning her flashlight around to see as many of the engine openings as she could. Nozzles showed in some, but not all.

"Looks like we're missing at least three engines, possibly more. I can't quite see the other side from here."

Paul turned to Deschamps. "What is the meaning of this? When you said 'not ready for flight,' you didn't say it was missing engines. What else is missing?"

Deschamps looked horrified. "I . . . Just a moment. Let me check the records." He had his omni out and was frantically tapping the screen to access the ship's maintenance database.

"Ah, here it is. Yes, four engines were removed for detailed inspection. One is in storage. We can reinstall that one for you, of course."

"And the other three?"

"That, er, that may be more difficult." Deschamps was visibly sweating now, and not from the heat. The hangar building was air-conditioned. He tapped his omni screen again.

Paul frowned. "The sales contract specifies that the *Jules Verne* is complete, except for the Interstellar Propulsion Module. Engines just don't disappear without work orders and a paper trail. Who authorized this, and why do the records at Transpatiale not reflect it?"

By now, Mary had crawled back out from under the *Verne*. "I remember something like that happening back at my home air-port. It turned out a maintenance guy had been playing a bit fast and loose with his parts sourcing, installing components from hangar queens but billing for new. Last I heard, he was still in jail, not just for the theft but also for reckless endangerment and falsi-fying maintenance records."

"The records have not been falsified!" Deschamps insisted, his glance darting from Mary to Paul and back to his omni screen. "Ah, here. Three were later installed on another vehicle."

"I still need three engines for the *Verne*," Paul said, his voice stern.

Rick, who had been silently observing the exchange, tapped Paul on the shoulder.

"What?" Paul said, irritated.

In a low voice, Rick said: "I have an idea about that. A word, if I may?"

Paul looked at him, then nodded. They stepped away, and Rick signaled Mary to join them.

"What is it?" Paul demanded.

"I'm thinking we want to upgrade the engines anyway," Rick said. "We're adding mass for the warp pods and internal fusors. It would be nice to have more thrust. Maybe swap them out for an upgrade?"

"Would that work?" Mary said. "They'd have to match the plumbing and the propellants."

"I think so. We can discuss the details back at the hotel."

Paul looked at his pilot. "Mary?"

"I'd have to run the numbers. And not just on the fuel ratios, I'd want to see if the *Verne* is structurally capable of dealing with the extra thrust and weight."

"It should be," Rick said, "but certainly, we'll get a Transpatiale engineer to check the calculations."

"All right," Paul said. "Let's look into that. Meanwhile, let's see if the *Verne* has any other surprises for us."

He turned back to Deschamps. "We will discuss the missing engines further. But for now, we want to take a look at the rest of the ship. Is ground power available? Mary will want to run some diagnostics." He glanced at her, and she nodded in agreement.

"Yes, of course," Deschamps said, obviously relieved to be off the hook, at least for now. He gestured to the technician. "*Vous. Connectez le véhicule à l'alimentation à quai. Vite!*" Connect the vehicle to shore power. Quickly!

Chapter 8: Ship Work

Hotel Atlantis, Kourou

The three of them, Paul, Mary, and Rick, gathered in Paul's room after dinner to discuss the day's findings.

"Well, what do you think?" Paul asked. "*Can* it be made spaceworthy?"

"I'll admit I had my doubts when I saw the missing engines," Mary said, "but they seem to have been cleanly uninstalled, with everything properly sealed off. The diagnostics were clean, no problems with the internal systems. On general principals, though, I'd want to flush the hydraulics, replace filters in the life support system, that kind of thing. But yes, if we replace the engines it will get us to space. Getting to another star is a different question. What do we do for a warp collar?"

"We'll get to that in a minute. Rick, any additional comments? You mentioned you had an idea about the engines?"

"Rather than just replace the missing three, I propose we swap them all out for something with improved performance. We could get a good deal on a set of lightly-used UltraRaptors, for example."

"Would that even work?" Mary said. "The propellant ratios aren't the same."

"They're close enough, and the UltraRaptor has a wide tolerance. It's actually a common upgrade, or it was until fusion-powered thrusters rendered chemical engines obsolete." Electric thrusters, powered by compact fusion reactors, were standard on new ships.

"But rockets aren't like Legos. You can't just mix and match parts from different vehicles."

Rick nodded. "Historically, you're right. There was very little design margin and everything had to be optimized. Not so true these days, and the UltraRaptor was designed with this kind of thing in mind."

"The engines, maybe," Mary said. "What about the rest of the *Jules Verne*? Will the structure take it?"

"Ah," Paul said. "This is something I asked Rick specifically to investigate. Not so much for the booster engines, but for the warp drive. As you pointed out, Mary, we have no warp collar."

"What does that have to do with the *Verne*'s structure? It's not like we're going to lift one to orbit, even if we had one."

With the original ships of the Alpha Centauri expedition, the warp pods, and the tokamak fusion reactor that powered them, were contained in a ring-shaped structure that surrounded the ship. These Interstellar Propulsion Modules, also known as IPMs or warp-collars, were assembled in orbit and then the landers—the *Poul Anderson*, *Krechet*, *Chandrasekhar*, and, initially, the *Jules Verne*—docked with them in space. (The non-landing ships *Robert Heinlein* and *Xing Hua* also had their warp modules affixed in space but were intended to stay that way, afterwards only ever landing on the Moon or similar light-gravity bodies.) After the expedition had departed, sans *Jules Verne,* China had repossessed its tokamak reactor, and the US reclaimed the warp pods.

"Quite so," Paul said. "We don't need a tokamak because we're using modern solid-state fusion reactors. They'll be inboard, partly replacing the *Verne*'s battery bank. Rick tells me the latest warp pods are smaller and lighter than the first versions. Rick, why don't you explain the idea?"

"Okay, right. Well, one of the weak points of original mission design was the need to leave the IPM in orbit, and to undock and dock with it."

"But you don't need it on the surface," Mary said. "You can't engage the warp in atmosphere, so it's just so much dead weight you're moving in and out of the planet's gravity well."

"Sure," Rick agreed, "but the new systems cut that mass tremendously, and you avoid the failure mode of not being able to re-dock with your warp collar. It also opens your launch window, eh? You don't have to synchronize with the collar's orbit."

"Okay, I'll buy that for now. Where do you put the warp modules? They have to be near the outside of the ship—look at the *Victoria* or *Vostok*, they had to stick the dorsal pod on a fin to get it far enough from the center of mass."

"Right, although part of that was for the artificial gravity geometry. We won't be doing that; it would put 'down' at ninety degrees to the current deck orientation."

"So, what will we be doing?"

"Six pods, like the original *Anderson* class, but smaller. Instead of mounting them on a separate ring, they'd be on the outside of the hull." Rick paused, gauging Mary's expression. She looked doubtful. "On retractable arms," he added, "so they don't mess up the aerodynamics too much during launch or descent."

Mary turned to Paul. "Is he *nuts*? Are you going along with this? What about the extra mass?"

"That's one reason I want to upgrade the engines," Rick said.

"He may well be nuts," Paul said, "but the idea has merit. Anyway, I'm not going to sign off on it until I see more analysis done. Rick already showed me a preliminary fluid-dynamics model showing that retracted pods won't, in fact, mess up the aerodynamics; they mostly snuggle in behind the shock waves, whichever way the ship is going. But I want to see structural analysis of the mounting points and the weight-and-balance calculation. The lower fuselage is reinforced for the landing legs anyway. The changes may be minor."

"And how long will these 'minor' changes take? Will there be enough time left to get to Delta Pavonis, look around, and get back in time for Fall term?"

"That's the question, isn't it?" Paul knew the schedule would be tight, and while he could probably arrange to take the term off, he wasn't sure about the others. "Based on what I know of the industry, and what Rick has told me, I think we can get it all done in less than three weeks, perhaps as little as two. But that's with engineering teams working twenty-four hours a day, and no hiccups in parts delivery. I hate having to do it, but I may have to wave my father's name around.

"That also means starting immediately, and we can't do *any* of that without formally taking possession of the *Verne*. So, shall I sign the deal, or do we look for another ship?"

"What are the chances of getting another ship?" Mary asked.

"Of buying one? Near zero for a used one, and there's a months-long waiting list for new, if we could even afford it. We *might* be able to charter something, but the only ship I'd heard of that might be coming available, a freighter on the Alpha Centauri run, had its contract extended. In any case, it would come with its own crew. That would mean you wouldn't get to fly it, Mary, and it would cost us extra."

"All right," she said. "Let's go with what we've got."

"Rick?" Paul felt sure he knew what the answer would be. He wondered if Rick realized what he was about to get himself into.

"Sure, let's do it."

"I'm glad you're so agreeable, Rick. You're now in charge of the refurb. I need you to track down those replacement engines and take responsibility for getting them installed. I have a line on the warp pods, but I need you to do the structural analysis and get those installed too. Don't do that yourself; hire it out. I'll give you a list of suitable companies. Call me if there are any problems or delays, or you have any questions."

"Call you? But where—"

"You will be staying here to oversee the work. I need to recruit a biologist and geologist, arrange for supplies, and chase down more funding. Especially that part."

"What am I doing?" Mary asked.

"For now, you're with Rick. He's in charge of the engines and structures. You mentioned refreshing the hydraulics and life support, so get that done. Also, get more training on the *Jules Verne*'s specific systems. There are technicians here who worked on them originally, so take advantage of that. Again, any questions or concerns, call me."

He looked from one to the other, slightly amused at the deer-in-the-headlights Rick had. He'd probably had the same look the first time—the first few times—his father had given him some new and seemingly overwhelming responsibility. Mary took it more calmly. She'd probably had similar responsibilities at the bush charter company back in the Arctic.

"Don't worry," he said, "I'm not abandoning you here in the jungle—" he looked around at the hotel suite pointedly, the Atlantis, while no luxury hotel, was actually a pretty nice place "—altogether. I'm not leaving until tomorrow night, and I'll be back in a few days. We'll do regular calls to stay in sync."

"Then what is our agenda for tomorrow?" Rick asked. "You need to deal with the transfer paperwork. What are Mary and I doing?"

Paul was going to suggest that they get started on their assigned tasks, then remembered that neither of them had been in Kourou before, and the past few days had been rushed.

"Sightseeing," he said. "Take part of the day and wander around Kourou. The beach is just over a kilometer away, although if you want to go swimming, I'd suggest the hotel pool. There's some kind of archeological museum, and of course the space museum. Rick, I do want you to get started on tracking those engines down. You can do that from anywhere; you've got your omniphone. Oh, and just so you know, there's a McDonald's less than a kilometer away; follow the road out here toward the beach then curve south before the traffic circle." The comment had more to do with Rick's food preferences than his last name. "At least, that's where it was when I was here as a kid. But really, there are much better restaurants."

"Yeah, Rick," Mary said, "we didn't come all this way to eat fast food."

"Fine, fine."

"*Bien.* I hope to be done with Deschamps by shortly after noon," Paul said, "then we can get back together and go over any last-minute details. But now, I think to bed. First thing in the morning, I have to go buy a starship."

Chapter 9: Progress Report

Several days later

Paul initiated the status update call after an exhausting day. He hoped Rick and Mary had made better progress than he had.

"*Bonjour*, how are things in Kourou?"

"Hot, humid, and mosquito-ey, at least outside," Rick replied. "But you probably want to know about our ship. That's going well. Deschamps has been most cooperative since you put the fear of God into him."

"Fear of my father, more like, but close enough." Paul hadn't made any actual threats; he wasn't in a position to, nor did he want to have to, but some strong hints in the wake of the fiasco of the missing engines had obviously helped.

"Right. Anyway, all the old engines have now been pulled, and the first of the replacements have been delivered. We're holding off on installing them to give us more working room for the other modifications. The warp pods have also arrived, and the technicians are checking them over. So far, so good, but we'll have to run final tests in space, of course."

"*Naturellement*." One didn't engage a warp field in atmosphere.

"By the way, I sent you the latest proposed changes. Have you had a chance to look at them?"

"I received them, but no, not yet. I will get to that after this call."

"Okay, I need your sign-off on those to order the parts fabbed."

"You'll get it by the morning. Either that, or I will call you tonight to tell you what you need to change."

"Uh, okay, fair enough."

"Mary, what about you?"

"The life support system has been overhauled. That was more of a chore than it should have been. It hadn't been properly cleaned out after the last flight."

"Ugh. I hope you complained."

"Of course I did, and Deschamps loaned me an extra tech to help with the job. I learned a lot from him, including some new swear words."

"Hah, I can imagine. What's next?"

"The forward electrics and hydraulics. We figured we save the aft systems until we're installing the warp pods, then make the necessary changes."

"Sensible," Paul said. "We are all on schedule then?"

"Currently, yes, at least as far as the ship goes," said Mary. "What's happening with recruiting the rest of the crew? You haven't said anything."

Paul sighed. "That is taking longer than I'd hoped. So far, most of the candidates have been heavy on lab work but with little or no field experience. That's not going to work for us. The names I have of people with that experience, well, most of them are unavailable. Some are already off-planet. Still, I'm talking to another biologist tomorrow. He comes recommended. He was a student of George Darwin, and apparently, he's looking for a new field project. His name is Corey Ogden, if that means anything to either of you?"

Neither Rick nor Mary had heard of him, but then they had no background in biology.

"No? Well, no matter. We also still need a geologist."

"Do we, though?" said Rick. "It's going to be biopharmacology where the real money is, not mining. Nobody ships ores or metals between stars."

"But we need a geologist's insight into processes on the planet. We also need an expert's opinion on the most valuable planetary data to collect, and how to collect it."

"I assume you've checked with the geology and mining departments on campus?" Mary asked.

"Of course, and on others besides. The same problem; it's either all lab experience, or they're out in the field. It doesn't help that field season has started already."

"Well, there's a geological exploration outfit I used to fly for up in northern Canada," Mary said. "I don't know that they'll have anyone available, but they might know someone."

"That is worth a try," Paul said. "Send me whatever contact information you have. I will follow up tomorrow. Anything else?"

"When are you coming back here?"

"I think as soon as I get the rest of the crew. I'd like to bring them down to see the ship and to meet you both. I'll make a final offer if it looks like they'll work out."

"And that answers the other question I had," Rick said. "Good. Talk again tomorrow?"

"*Oui*, unless I have questions about your proposal tonight. *À bientôt*."

∞ ∞ ∞

Kingston, Ontario

From his resume, the biologist candidate, Dr. Corey Ogden, looked like a good fit. With a PhD in Comparative Biology, his broad background, covering everything from anatomy to zoology, with exposure to microbiology, paleontology, and, as a former student of George Darwin, exobiology, seemed an ideal fit for an expedition with limited resources. He also had broad field experience.

Paul set up an interview via omniphone. They could meet in person if it went well.

∞ ∞ ∞

"So, why would you want to come on this expedition?" Paul had asked him after the usual questions. "It's risky, and we might not even find anything."

"But it sounds like a fantastic opportunity," Corey said. "To be honest, I get bored easily. That's one reason I went into comparative biology. I couldn't decide on any one specialty, and it seemed a good mix. Worst case, if we get to Delta Pavonis and find that green planet uninhabitable and devoid of life—although that's unlikely, from what you've told me—I get to put down the interstellar trip on my resume, which makes me a better candidate for the next expedition."

Paul appreciated the man's forward thinking. "And the risk?"

"If there's one thing that the study of life has taught me, it's that death comes to us all. I could slip in the shower and crack my skull open tomorrow. Life *is* risk; it's just a matter of managing it appropriately. If you've learned anything from your father —yes, I looked up your history—it's that you're not afraid to take risks, but you don't take stupid ones. Is that a fair statement?"

Paul had started to bristle at the mention of his father, but he realized that Corey was right, and very perceptive. "*Oui*, I like to think it is. I'd like to invite you to meet the rest of the team. They're in Kourou, getting our ship ready."

"French Guiana? Certainly. When?"

"Sooner would be better. When are you available?"

Corey grinned. "Would tomorrow work?"

Paul hadn't expected that. "The day after would work better. I'm still looking for a geologist, and I'd like to bring both of you down at the same time, but I can be flexible on that."

"Do you have somebody in mind? I may know someone."

"I have some names. So far, I've had no luck on availability."

"Here," Corey said, beaming the contact information over the omniphone link. "Kristen Payne. We took a paleontology class together, but she's a field geologist, and a good one. I think she's available. The sponsorship for her summer field trip fell through."

Paul peered at Ogden's screen image, considering. This could be exactly what he needed, or it could be a source of problems. "You have a personal relationship with Dr. Payne?"

"What? Oh, no, nothing like that. We're friends and former classmates, is all. We keep in touch, but we're not close."

"*Bon*. Well, thank you, I will add her to my list. Speaking of which, I have calls to make. If you're agreeable, I will contact you about travel arrangements to Kourou. If there's nothing else. . . ?"

Corey took the hint. "Not right now. I'll call if I have questions. *Merci beaucoup*, *Monsieur* Fabron."

Paul guessed from the accent that that was probably the extent of Ogden's French, but let it slide. That wasn't what he was being hired for.

∞ ∞ ∞

Paul followed up on some of the other names on his list, with the same unsatisfactory results as what he'd had so far, before contacting Dr. Kristen Payne. It turned out that she was indeed available, and Paul liked what he saw in her resume.

"Are you sure you don't want a planetologist?" she asked during the phone interview. "I mean, I know the basics, of course, but that's not my focus."

"I have an astrophysicist," Paul said, somewhat exaggerating Rick's qualifications. "I'm not that concerned with planet's formation. What I need is someone qualified to give us some geological insight into the planet's surface, identify places to collect representative samples, and maybe give some insight as to the planet's history over the past sixty-five million years. Especially as it may have influenced evolution on the planet."

"So you're pretty sure it's been terraformed," she said. He hadn't told her that, nor their specific destination. That she had figured it out from his question was a point in her favor.

"That's what we hope to find out. Is that something you feel capable of?"

"If I have the right equipment, both on the ground and either in orbit or aerial survey, then yes."

"We won't have an anti-neutrino scanner—" the first Alpha Centauri mission had had one, it could image the interior of a planet like a CAT scan, but required a fission reactor as the anti-neutrino source "—but make a list of what you would need and prioritize it by essential versus nice-to-have. We'll see what we can do."

"That's fine. I can do without an ANT-scan," she said. "I'll send you the list. Do I take it that means you're interested?"

"*Oui*, so far, so good. Just a few more details."

By the end of the interview, he had arranged to have her meet him and Corey for the trip to Kourou.

Chapter 10: Launch Day

Kourou Spaceport, French Guiana

The entire crew had been in Kourou for the past three days now. The science team—primarily Corey Ogden and Kristen Payne, with Rick McDonald pulling double duty as the astrophysicist as well as the ship's engineer—had been ensuring that all their instruments and supplies had been received and were properly stowed.

Mary, with Rick's assistance, had made sure the *Jules Verne*'s systems were all functional. That had included having the *Verne* rolled out to the launch pad, fueled, and clamped down while the engines were fired in a static test. Mary was mildly amused at the whole idea. This would be the last time the *Verne* ever launched from an actual launch pad, with the rest of the trip "in the wild," as it were. True, Kakuloa at Alpha Centauri had a landing field, but it was primarily designed for newer ships; there would be no launch pad facility for the likes of *Jules Verne*.

Paul, of course, had run himself ragged making sure that all the above was taken care of, liaising with the spaceport authorities, and making final arrangements for the ground-side component of Paon Co.—a part-time business manager—to operate in their absence, including making additional licensing or data purchase arrangements for whatever they might find.

Finally, they were ready for launch.

∞ ∞ ∞

"Kourou Control, this is *Jules Verne*," Mary called over the comm circuit, "ship is on internal power, and valves are closing to pressurize. Commence drain-back." It was two minutes to launch. Any propellants remaining in the umbilical tower hoses were now draining back to the storage tanks.

"Confirm internal power and drainback. T-minus 100 seconds."

At T-90, the *Verne*'s internal computers would take over the show from Kourou Control's. It could still abort if it detected a problem, or by emergency override from ground control, but the odds of that were small.

"*Jules Verne*, T-minus 90, you are GO for launch."

"Thank you Control, confirm GO. Computers on internal."

The launch umbilical tower began to retreat from the rocket. It had hardly been necessary, the squat vehicle could stand fine on its own, and the propellent, communications, and power connectors were all near the base. The walkway to the *Verne*'s hatch had been handy, though. On the rest of the trip, they'd be using the ladder.

"All right, people, this is it," Paul announced on the internal comm circuit. "One minute to launch. I hope you all remembered to check out of your rooms at the Atlantis." That got a chuckle from someone on the circuit, helping to relieve the prelaunch tension.

There were several loud clicks and thumps, and the volume level of the background hiss of venting gases rose. "Engine prechill start," Mary announced. "T-minus 30."

She kept her eyes on her screens, watching the countdown clock at one corner while scanning the instruments. The computers would notice anything suddenly out of range before she did, but a human could sometimes still catch an unusual trend in the readings before even a good AI could.

"All right, here we go. T minus ten, nine, eight, seven, six, five—" The engine sounds increased as the intakes came fully open and the pre-burners lit with a low rumble, rapidly increasing in pitch as the turbines spooled up. "—two, one—" The thundering roar of all engines coming to full thrust drowned out her "zero." The vehicle shook for a moment as the computers verified everything was running correctly, then Mary and the rest were pushed back into their seats as the hold-down clamps released and the *Jules Verne* lumbered toward space.

"And liftoff!"

∞ ∞ ∞

The flight was, as old space hands sometimes put it, "norminal," both normal and nominal. In fact, it might have been better than that.

To transit the relatively crowded region of Near-Earth Orbit, they needed to stick to a specific flight plan. They had launched into a designated 300-kilometer orbit. After on-orbit diagnostic checks, they got clearance for a one-millisecond warp hop to a point, well out of the orbital plane of the Moon and most satellite traffic, for final calibration of the warp system.

That one-millisecond warp was too short for Rick to say with certainty, but he thought it might be slightly more efficient than their original estimates. "It's down in the third decimal place," he said. "I'll know better when we do some longer jumps after we stop off at Luna."

Their short stay on the Moon was similarly uneventful, and after a brief exchange of formalities they were ready for deeper space.

They did their jumps, Rick verified their position and timing for each one, and confirmed it. "We're one-point-two percent faster than anticipated, and we used less fuel. Our net is about three percent more efficient. Mary, shorten the jump to Alpha Centauri. We don't want to overshoot."

"Don't worry, we'll be stopping well short of the system to plan our approach," she said.

"Excellent," Paul said. "Mary, whenever you're ready, let's head for Alpha Centauri."

"Aye, Captain," Mary said, grinning. "People, prepare for a couple of days of boredom; there won't be anything to see out the windows."

"*Non, non*. We won't get too bored. We have to exercise to keep fit in the zero-gee, and we have all the reports of the Alpha Centauri missions to read through, and whatever others I could get hold of. I want us prepared."

At the expected groans, he smiled and added, "Plus, the ship's library also has a collection of books, films, and games. But study first, play later."

"Is it too early to stage a mutiny?" Rick wondered aloud, but he was smiling. To him, reading the mission reports would be almost as entertaining as anything else.

"Can we go now?" Mary asked.

"Of course." Paul caught Rick's eye and grinned. He raised his arm and made a sweeping, forward-pointing gesture. "Engage!"

Mary rolled her eyes, but pushed the button.

Part II - Outbound

Chapter II: Alpha Centauri

Alpha Centauri System

The *Jules Verne* came out of warp ten AU from Alpha Centauri B, Kakuloa's sun.

"We're here," Mary said. "Now what?"

"The spaceport at Krechet's Landing is where we can top up our deuterium tanks," Paul said. "We'll need to contact them, of course. What's the standard procedure?"

"As you say, we contact them and give them a heads up. But right now, we're over a light-hour from the planet. We should get in closer."

"Any radio traffic now?"

She glanced at the RF spectrum analyzer. "Nothing on the general channels. There's some chatter on private bands."

"All right. Whatever the standard approach is, then."

Mary calibrated a short jump to one AU from Kakuloa. There, they picked up a broadcast from a navigation beacon.

"*. . . ships in-bound for Kakuloa: Proceed with caution to the Kakuloa-Mahina Nui L5 point and contact approach. Ships from Earth or Sawyer's World may contact Kakuloa directly. Ships arriving from any other terraformed or life-bearing planet must contact the Quarantine Directorate at Mahina Nui for further instructions.*" There was a pause, then the message began to repeat, "*This broadcast is for all ships in-bound for Kakuloa: Proceed with—*" she cut it off.

"So, proceed to L5."

"What does 'with caution' mean?"

"It means don't be a hot dog and try to jump directly to it at maximum warp. That would be a fool thing to do anyway; other ships aside, the L5 points can accumulate debris. So, I reduce speed by making small, millisecond warp jumps, in between which we watch where we're going." She looked over the navigation panel. "We should be there in twenty minutes."

"Sounds good."

There were no other ships when the *Verne* reached the designated L5 point, at least none near enough to see or to show up on radar.

Mary looked over at Paul. "Do you want to do the honors, Captain?"

"Thank you, yes." He activated his microphone and the radio. "Kakuloa Control, this the starship *Jules Verne*, out of Earth, Paul Fabron commanding. We are holding at L5 and request landing instructions for Krechet Field."

There was silence in response. Paul looked over at Mary quizzically.

"Two-second radio delay," she reminded him.

"Ah, *oui*."

"Jules Verne, *this is Kakuloa. Do a tangential warp to 500 km altitude over the eastern horizon from your position. Uploading coordinates now. That will set you up for entry and descent. Contact us again when in position. The field is currently clear for the next several hours. I'm not familiar with your ship; do you have any special landing needs?*"

"Coordinates acknowledged, Kakuloa. *Verne* is a modified *Anderson* class," Paul grinned, wishing he could be in the control room to see their reaction when they heard that. "After entry, we'll be doing a vertical descent from ten thousand meters, if that's all right with you."

"Anderson *class? You're* that Jules Verne*? Uh, roger that. Contact to confirm parameters prior to entry and descent. And, even if you are a few years late, let me be the first to welcome you to Alpha Centauri.*"

"Copy that, and *merci.*"

"Well, you got their attention," Mary said.

"What did he mean, a few years late?" Kristen asked.

"I thought you all knew the story? This ship was supposed to be part of the original Drake expedition to Alpha Centauri, the first one. When it wasn't ready in time, nobody wanted to wait."

"So why didn't it go back for the *Anderson* crew? It must have been ready by then."

"It wasn't. The Chinese had reclaimed their fusion reactor. That turned out well for us. We couldn't have gotten the *Verne* so cheap if it hadn't been sitting in mothballs for the past eight years."

"Hangar queen," Mary muttered. She had been working at the console as they talked. With a final check, she said, "I have the course for our entry point laid in. Shall we?"

"*Une moment.*" Paul looked around at everyone floating in the control area. "*Ecoutez.* One more warp to just above the atmosphere and then we begin our descent. Go back to your positions and strap in. Tray tables and seatbacks in the upright position, people."

After an echo of boos and moans at the lame joke, Corey and Kristen headed back to the lower deck as the others took to their seats. A few moments later, Corey called back, "All right, we're ready, let's go."

Paul turned to Mary. "You heard him. Let's go."

∞ ∞ ∞

Krechet's Landing, Kakuloa

The warp pod retraction went without incident, as did the descent and landing at Krechet Field.

They could see the old *Krechet* itself, looking decidedly more worn and weather-beaten than the *Verne*, at one edge of the field. Two newer V-class ships were also parked along one edge, and beyond the landing area itself, near the beach, lay the growing resort complex of Kakuloa City.

"Will we get a chance to visit the resort?" Rick asked.

"My plan was pretty much just to refuel and get going, but that was before spending the better part of a week cooped up in the ship. We can take a sightseeing day, but I don't know if the resort is operational yet. But first we have to clear it with the Colony Administrator." At that moment, the incoming comm signal light started blinking. "That's probably him now."

"This is the *Jules Verne*, Fabron speaking."

"*Captain Fabron, this is William Blake. I must say we're all a little surprised to see your ship. You had quite an audience watching your landing.*"

"My apologies if we caused any disruption, Administrator Blake. That wasn't our intention."

"*Not at all, we can use a little excitement from time to time. But we do have some formalities to take care of. Shall I come up or would you like to meet me in my office?*"

"If you wouldn't mind, Mr. Blake, why don't you come up. This ship doesn't have artificial gravity, so I'd like to give us all a little while to adjust before climbing down the ladder."

"*I'd be happy to, and I think I can arrange a gantry for you. I'll be over shortly.*"

∞ ∞ ∞

Administrator's Office

Blake closed the commlink to the *Verne*, and immediately called to his aide.

"Gene, I'm going to go out to meet them. Find me a mobile gantry or cherry picker or something that will reach that hatch. I don't mind climbing the ladder, but that crew has been in zero-gee for the last few days. I'd rather not have anyone falling. Also, find out anything you can on a Paul Fabron, and anything recent we have on the *Jules Verne*. They didn't get that ship spaceworthy overnight; there must have been some news in the last few weeks."

"Already on it," his aide said. "Take a look at the VERNE file on your desktop. And the Operations Chief is rounding up a driver for the cherry picker."

"Excellent work, as always."

Blake took a moment to transfer the VERNE file to his omni. There wasn't much. Any news of the ship actually leaving the solar system wouldn't arrive until the next courier run, unless the *Jules Verne* itself was courier rated, which he doubted.

He scanned it as he walked out of the office and to the vehicle shed where a driver had just pulled around an electric truck, one of the bigger vehicles in the spaceport. It was topped by a folding, extensible boom with an attached basket big enough for three or four people. It was usually used more for working on the upper surface of V-class ships, or on their dorsal warp pods. It could reach up and over without touching the rest of the ship. It would easily extend upward to the hatch of the *Jules Verne*, and in fact it was occasionally used for inspection and routine maintenance of the *Krechet*, now designated a historic monument.

"Excellent, let's go," Blake said as he climbed up to join the driver in the cab.

The *Verne* had landed on the far side of the field. It couldn't maneuver on the ground the way newer ships could, and Blake had wanted to keep most of the field clear for other arriving ships, although there was nothing scheduled until the day after tomorrow.

Blake noticed something different about the *Jules Verne*. He glanced back toward the *Krechet*, anchored at the far side of the field, then again at the *Verne*. Yes, the *Verne* had cylinders mounted around its waist, almost like old-time SRBs, solid rocket boosters, but they had no nozzles. Auxiliary fuel tanks for longer range? They didn't look big enough. *Warp pods*, perhaps?

By now, any heat from the landing thrusters had dissipated, and the truck drove up beside the forward landing leg. The ladder had already been extended, and Blake noted that the hatch door stood open, with a safety chain fastened across the open doorway.

Blake and the driver climbed out of the truck cab and up into the basket. The basket was an open style, more a platform with a fence-like railing on all four sides, with an inward-opening gate at the front. Beside the gate was a small control panel.

"You might want to grab the rail," the driver/operator said. "It can shake a bit when it's moving."

Blake did so while the operator switched on the control panel and checked the status lights. From below came the whine of the electric pump pressurizing the hydraulics. The operator grabbed one of the small joysticks built into the console and held the railing with his other hand. "Up we go."

With a slight wobble, the folded arm straightened out like a person reaching above his head. Blake gripped the railing. He had no problem with heights, having flown in all manner of aircraft, but this was a new experience.

"Ahoy *Jules Verne*," he called to the open hatchway.

A young man stepped out of the shadow of the airlock and up to the safety chain. He couldn't have been more than his early twenties, if that.

"*Bonjour*!" he called. "Mr. Blake, I presume?"

The operator brought the cage forward toward the open door, stopping it just centimeters shy of the ship.

"I am. And you are Captain Paul Fabron?" At the young man's nod, Blake continued. "Permission to come aboard?"

"By all means." He unsnapped the safety chain and extended a hand to Blake, who shook it, then he opened the cage's own gate and stepped aboard.

"Welcome to Kakuloa," Blake said. "What brings you here?"

"Several things," Fabron said, gesturing Blake to follow him into the ship. "First, as your Space Traffic Controller surmised, I thought it was time the *Jules Verne* completed the trip she never got a chance to make back in '69. That mission is now accomplished."

They made their way into the ship and up to the bridge. Although Blake had never flown on one of these ships, he was familiar with the layout. He wondered about the rest of the crew.

There was no way Fabron had flown this solo, but there were cabins on the lower deck. The crew members were probably resting there. As they reached the bridge, he saw a woman sitting at the controls. She looked older than Fabron, but still young, perhaps not yet thirty. She had a slightly Asian look, but one Blake couldn't place.

Fabron introduced her. "This is Mary Kalvak, my pilot and first officer. We're not big on rank; it's a private ship. Mary, Administrator Blake."

"William Blake. I have no problem with keeping things informal. And the rest of your crew?"

"Five total. Just a moment." He touched a control. "Come on up to the bridge and introduce yourselves, people. Don't be shy."

Blake heard commotion below. He looked at Fabron. "You mentioned several reasons for this trip. What else?"

"We need to refuel. We've got a couple of long jumps ahead of us. And we'd like to take a day or two to see the sights here, if that's possible."

"Fuel is no problem. As far as seeing the sights, there's the beach, but the resort isn't officially open yet."

"Ah, I was afraid of that."

"However, the owner, Parry Cohen, is on planet. He's usually eager to show people around if he's not in the middle of something. Perhaps I can introduce you. Are you connected with Fabron Industries, by any chance?" Blake had picked that up from the file.

The young man sighed. "Yes. My father. I would rather you didn't let that influence anything one way or the other. He's not connected with this venture."

The others had come up the gangway to the bridge, and were waiting at a respectful distance, as best they could in the limited space. They all looked young, with perhaps one other Mary's age. *Or maybe I'm just getting old*, Blake reflected. Half the crew of the first expedition had been barely into their thirties, but these looked even younger.

He turned back to Fabron. "And what venture is that?"

The young man paused, as if deciding whether or not to tell him. "I think we have enough of a head start," he said, "but I ask for discretion."

Blake didn't see any harm in that. "So long as it's nothing illegal, you have it."

"*Bon.* You're looking at the Paon Company. We're going to Delta Pavonis. We believe it has a terraformed planet, and we intend to be first to explore it."

Oh, good grief, Blake thought to himself. *Kids on a joy ride.* And he realized there was nothing, legally, he could do to stop them.

∞ ∞ ∞

Krechet's Landing

Blake cleared the paperwork for the five crew of the *Jules Verne*, paying particular attention to assure that they were, in fact, all crew and were voluntarily part of the mission; that Mary Kalvak was a fully qualified starship pilot, a new one, true, but her experience on in-atmosphere craft was impressive; and that the documentation for the ship itself was in order. He wouldn't be able to hold up their journey on a technicality.

While the others caught a ride in the boom lift truck back to the spaceport reception area, William Blake invited Paul Fabron to accompany him in an aircar down to Kakuloa City to meet with Parry Cohen.

On the way there, Blake flew the car around the old *Krechet*, still leaning at a slight angle where one landing leg had broken through the rock ceiling of an old lava tube in the basalt, now held in place by guy wires and a supporting post under the leg.

"This is one of your sister ships," Blake said as he pointed it out. "The *Anderson,* of course, is on Sawyer's World. It's in worse shape, sitting at a forty-degree angle after stampeding girannos knocked it over. This class of ship is a bit top heavy with the tanks empty, something to keep in mind."

"Yes," Paul said. "They did mention that in training. We intend to fill the tanks as soon as possible after landing."

"I wondered about that. How? The *Krechet*, and the *Anderson* for that matter, are still where they are because they didn't have their separate refueling modules. Do you?"

"It's built in. Thanks to improvements in fusion technology, we have a compact module on board that will power the fuel processor. It also powers our warp pods."

"The bulges on the side of your ship?" Blake said. "I wondered if that's what those were. That's quite a change from the thick donuts the original mission used."

"Yes, most of that was the tokamak, which we don't need. We borrowed the idea from your V-class ships. Much easier than leaving the warp ring in orbit and worrying about docking."

"Good idea."

Blake tilted the aircar away from the *Krechet* and toward the towers of Kakuloa City. From the outside, the buildings were complete, but Blake knew a lot of finishing remained to be done on the interiors.

"Tell me, Mr. Blake, why did you show me this?" Paul gestured back to the *Krechet*.

"I just thought you'd be interested. Why?"

"You weren't trying to scare me?"

Blake considered his reply. He supposed he had been, a little. Not that he wanted to admit that. And young as the crew of the *Jules Verne* were, they were all adults. Hell, Blake himself had joined the armed services at a younger age than them. "In a way, yes," he finally said, "but don't take it personally, I try to scare everyone who comes out here for the first time. I want to make sure you recognize, really recognize, some of the potential dangers you're taking your crew into. Earth has become a surprisingly safe place, more than many people who come out here realize." He waved his arm at the beach. "That looks pretty, and so far, we haven't found any sharks in Kakuloan waters, but there are still creatures that will eat you or sting you to death. However nice it may look, it's not a park, although Cohen is doing his best to make sure this stretch of beach is safe."

Paul nodded, looking out at the beach, and the clear waters beyond. "Yes, it's not good to upset the paying customers. You might want to tone your sales pitch back for the tourists." He turned back to Blake, turning more serious. "I understand more than you realize. My father travelled to some interesting places when he was growing his business, and I often went with him. I had a bodyguard until I turned twelve, for fear of kidnappings. I almost *was* kidnapped. Twice. I earned my black belt in martial arts at twelve, and became an expert shot with a pistol. Then we started living in more civilized places."

Blake was impressed, but unfazed. He looked Paul in the eye, trusting the car's autopilot for a moment. "That's all very well for you, and I'm glad to hear it. But what about your crew? You're the leader of your expedition, which means you are responsible for each of them. Are they up to it? Are you?"

The aircar descended to the parking area near the resort construction offices, and Blake shut it down. "Come on," he said, climbing out, "let's go meet Perry Cohen. I warn you, he's a bit of a character."

∞ ∞ ∞

Kakuloa Resort

Blake had contacted Cohen and explained the situation, swearing him to secrecy regarding the *Verne*'s ultimate destination. Cohen had been eager to meet the young Fabron, and while the hotel wasn't completely finished, one floor had accommodations available for contractors and others with business at the resort. He was willing to put the Paon Company up in exchange for some publicity photographs.

"We might not use the pictures, of course," Cohen explained, "but the *Jules Verne* is a historic ship, and if you do find another terraformed planet at Delta Pavonis, it will be doubly so, and having its crew stop here on the way there would be something to brag about."

"I don't see a problem with that, Mr. Cohen," Paul said as they discussed it, "just so long as you stick to the NDA until we return."

"Of course, and call me Parry, please."

"And I'm Paul. I'm sorry, was it Perry or Parry? I'm not sure I heard correctly. Sometimes I have trouble with accents."

"Parry is a nickname. Long story, but part of it is that I used to be on a fencing team. And your English is far better than my French, er, *votre anglais est plus bien que mon français.*"

Paul suppressed a wince at Parry's accent. "Not at all," he said graciously, "but let's keep it in English for everyone else's sake."

"Of course. And listen, has anyone discussed resort options with you?"

"What do you mean? I don't think we're ready to invest here just yet. Perhaps when the company has grown."

"That's not what I meant, although I'd be happy to discuss that when you're ready. No, I understand that it's early, you haven't even reached Delta Pavonis yet, but if it does turn out to be terraformed and have some attractive locations on it, I'd like to get in on the ground floor. What do you say? I'll waive any room and meal fees here at the hotel for you and your company in exchange for a share in any resort rights DPC has in whatever you discover."

Paul smiled. He was beginning to understand how Cohen had gotten where he was. "That's a very interesting offer, Mr. Cohen, I mean, Parry, considering we haven't discovered anything yet. On the other hand, unless I'm mistaken, this hotel isn't certified for guest occupancy yet, so you can't actually charge fees for anyone staying here."

"Ah, well—"

"And even if you could," Paul continued, "that seems a small investment for an actual share in resort rights. But you're certainly entitled to something in exchange for your generosity. I think I can persuade the company to give you an option to buy shares of those rights at a favorable rate. How does that sound?"

"It sounds like you take after your father," Parry said with a grin, "or at least, what I've heard from his reputation. What the heck, even if it turns out as bad as Epsilon Eridani, in an ice age with savage animals, I'm not out much. You've got a deal." He held out his hand, and he and Paul shook on it.

"You never know," Paul added, "there's probably a market for adventure tourists to go look at the savage animals."

Cohen chuckled. "There might be, at that."

∞ ∞ ∞

Paul thought about that as he left Cohen to meet with the others. Any terraformed planet would inevitably have savage animals. Kakuloa had something like crocodiles nearby, and almost certainly worse back in the still largely unexplored forests. Sawyer's World certainly did; girannos and terror birds and big cats had come close to killing various members of the *Anderson* crew. Even small creatures could be dangerous if they had a toxic bite or sting. He'd even seen a report on rumors that the Chinese had lost a crewman to an animal attack at Epsilon Eridani; although details were lacking, the rumors were likely true.

They would have to exercise caution at Delta Pavonis. He knew he and Mary were both skilled with firearms, and to hear her tell it, Mary had faced down more than one polar bear. His team all had camping experience and some survival training, that had been a prerequisite, but it might not be enough. Fortunately, he had already made plans to pick up firearms here on Kakuloa, rather than going through the necessary paperwork on Earth. Some things were easier on the frontier.

Chapter 12: The Other Guys

Earth

"How soon can the *Matthew* be ready for deep space?" Edward Talbot demanded of Sebastian Thorne, his second in command.

"Physically, she's ready now. We need to finish loading supplies, then just fuel and go."

"Is that hours, days, or what?"

"A week. There's a supply delivery scheduled to lift three days from now. Give it a day to get to the Moon—" the *Matthew* was currently parked near the lunar quarantine station after its post-maintenance test flight—"and a couple of days to transfer the cargo. Fueling only takes as little as an hour, but we have to reserve ahead of time to make sure there's a supply on hand. Is there some rush?"

"Yes. Fabron's team has already launched. They left without fanfare three days ago. They'll be at Alpha Centauri by now."

"On what ship? I thought there weren't any available." The *Matthew* itself had had some of its scheduled, but less critical, maintenance deferred to make it available.

"The *Jules Verne*. They'd been quietly refitting it. I guess nobody pays much attention to what's going on in French Guiana."

"The *Verne*? That won't have the range to reach Delta Pavonis from Alpha Centauri, surely?" Even the *Matthew*, with its longer-range tanks and more-efficient engines, couldn't quite manage it.

"They've upgraded the *Verne*'s systems, but I doubt by that much. If they can get ten light years out of her, they could go via Epsilon Indi, same as us."

"We've got the range to make it direct to Epsilon Indi, so we don't need to go via Alpha Centauri." Thorne did some quick mental arithmetic. "It would cut two light years off the trip, so if we left today, we could easily beat them."

"We can't. We have cargo to deliver to Kakuloa, we don't have clearance to go direct to E-Indi, and you said yourself, we don't have all our supplies loaded."

"Let's hope they decide to spend a couple of days on the beach at Kakuloa, then. But they'll be taking some time on the way to calibrate their warp drive, right? Those old *Anderson*-class ships were considerably slower, too, right? We could still get there first."

"If we don't dawdle, and if they haven't upgraded their warp drive. Can we be ready to depart in two days?"

"Two days? I don't see how. We'd have to leave for the Moon by tomorrow. I don't know if there's a flight available, and we still need to get supplies loaded."

"Can we do without the supplies? The *Matthew* has some already loaded, right?"

"It does, but not enough," Thorne said. "Air and water will be fine, those recycle, but we'll be running out of food for the return trip. There's survey gear we might be missing, too."

Talbot muttered to himself. The contracts required at least a basic survey. If they didn't have the gear for that, there was little point to the mission.

"Make sure we have at least the minimum gear we need, however you have to get it. I'll find us a flight. Be ready to get it loaded with whatever you can before liftoff. As far as food goes, we can pick up extra at Kakuloa. If we do have to tighten our belts on the way back, or cut the trip short, we'll do it. If the planet *is* terraformed, we can find something to feed to the food processors. Those *are* installed, right?"

"Uh, yes, sir."

"Then do it. I'll signal you the flight details as soon as I have them."

"Do you even know the departure spaceport?"

"No. Assume anyplace launching to Luna. Get redundant cargoes ready, one at each port until you hear from me."

"But the cost. . . ."

"We'll worry about that later. That's nothing to the billions an exclusive on a new terraformed planet could be worth." Or it could ruin him if there were no terraformed planet, or if it had no useful resources, or Fabron managed to claim it first. Baylor was backing him, yes, but Talbot knew he had exceeded his authority here. No matter, he hadn't gotten to his current position by playing it too safe.

"Maybe I can arrange a deal on supplies already on Luna. Buy them now with the promise to replace them in a week." Thorne said. "It would let us load immediately."

"If so, do it. Whatever it takes. Now go!"

As Thorne scurried out of the office, Talbot set about looking for the next flight to the Moon he could book for himself, the rest of his crew, and several hundred kilograms of gear and supplies.

Chapter 13: Leaving Kakuloa

Administrator Blake's office, Kakuloa

"All right," said Blake to Paul Fabron and Mary Kalvak, gathered in his office for a final, pre-departure, briefing. "This is from me as the ranking *UDT* official on Kakuloa, not as the Colony Administrator. Understood?"

"What difference does it make?" Paul asked.

"As Colony Administrator, my concern is only what happens on Kakuloa. As a *UDT* official, my concern is anything involving citizens of *UDT* countries, which you both are, anywhere *UDT* regulations cover. Which includes not only Kakuloa, but everywhere else in outer space, including both the Epsilon Indi and Delta Pavonis systems."

"That's a bit grabby, isn't it?" Mary said. "And what about Sawyer's World?"

Blake scowled. This conversation was not going in the direction he intended. "Sawyer's World is covered by the Treaty of Alpha Centauri and is irrelevant to this discussion. If you end up going there, talk it over with officials there. As for being 'grabby,' as you put it, nobody is claiming those systems, as such, because the Outer Space Treaty forbids such claims. We're just saying that if you break *UDT* laws, even if you're on the far side of the galaxy, you're answerable to the *UDT*. Is *that* understood?"

"Yes, of course," said Paul, "but what is your point? We're not planning to break any laws."

"No," Blake said, "I'm sure you aren't, at least, not any laws that you're aware of. I just want to make sure that you know about certain rules that apply to where you're going."

"All right then. We're all ears."

"First and foremost, quarantine regulations. You probably already know this, but if you touch down on a terraformed world, or for that matter any world with potential life on it, terraformed or not, you're not allowed to land back on Earth, or here, or for that matter, Sawyer's World, without landing on its moon first for decontamination and quarantine."

"Yes, we know that. It seems a bit excessive, but we understand."

"Good. That brings me to the second point. Any biological specimens you bring back, live or dead, have to be kept isolated and must be declared when you return—"

"Mr. Blake, we're quite familiar with the quarantine directorate's regulations, and we certainly intend to comply with them. We have a biologist on the crew. And we're also familiar with the regulations concerning forward contamination as well as back contamination. We all had to pass tests on those regulations. Can we just take it as read that we understand all that?"

Blake hesitated, but the truth was he didn't feel like wasting any more time on that than they did.

"I'm sorry, you're right," he said. "This is a new situation. Up until now, all exploration has been done by government-supervised crews and ships. Even the *Victoria*, owned and operated by Centauri Pharmaceuticals, was under my command once it landed here. To my knowledge, you're the first all-private ship and crew to go exploring new planets. You won't be the last . . . unless you have some royal screw up. In that case, expect the *UDT* to come down hard on any potential private venture out here, which will hold back mankind's expansion to the stars for decades, at least. I don't want that, and I'm sure you don't want that, and especially you don't want the liability that would go along with such a screw up. And don't expect the limited liability nature of your company to help there. They'd come after you personally for any violated regulations or negligence. That's assuming you make it back at all."

Neither Paul nor Mary said anything for a few moments, digesting what Blake had said.

"Are you trying to scare us again, Mr. Blake?" Paul finally asked.

"No, I'm just laying out the facts. If they scare you, then perhaps you're not ready to make this trip. If they encourage you to follow procedures and take appropriate precautions, then my job is done. Almost done."

"Almost?"

"There's one other thing regarding Epsilon Indi. There's some information about the planet that is currently being withheld. It surprised me when the *Grande Hermine* returned here from there a few months ago."

"About the planet Taprobane, you mean? We know that it's terraformed, and we have the physical data. There was no particular warning against airborne toxins or virulent bacteria. Wouldn't dangerous lifeforms be mentioned?"

"That would probably depend," Blake said, "on whether they were encountered near the landing area, or how extensive a survey the ship did. But in this case, the answer is no."

"Then there *is* a dangerous lifeform? Can't we just pick a landing area where it's not found?"

"Oh, you are required to do that. I'll give you data on allowable landing areas, although there should be a beacon in the system transmitting that information also."

Paul looked at Mary, then back at Blake. "Okay. Why is this lifeform so dangerous anyway?"

"It's intelligent . . . and has a civilization."

"*What?*"

"The *Grande Hermine* avoided contact, but from their surveys, they estimated a roughly iron-age level of civilization, with the more advanced towns and villages like early medieval Europe. There were also more primitive villages elsewhere. *UDT* is still trying to figure out how to make contact with the Taprobani natives—they're calling the species *timoans* for now—and how to release the news to the public at large. It's less of a secret out here, as there have been leaks. People who have lived off-Earth for a while know that most Earthers wouldn't understand what life is like."

Mary Kalvak spoke up. "I get it. I grew up in Nunavut, northern Canada. Nobody in the rest of the country, well, the south, understands what living on a frontier is like."

"Exactly," Blake said, "except that the Canadian arctic, even the bush, is civilized compared to out here."

"So, when we land on Taprobane to refuel, don't talk to the native timoans. Got it," Paul said.

"Don't even be *seen* by the natives," Blake said. "You may not be the only ship in the system. Epsilon Indi is close enough to Sol that some of the newer ships can make the trip directly, so the traffic wouldn't come through here. I know the *UDT* has been planning some more discreet surveys, but I don't know the schedule. If there *are* Space Force ships in the system, heed their instructions, and you should be fine."

Paul and Mary looked at each other without saying anything. Paul raised an eyebrow, and Mary gave him a slight nod in return. He turned back to Blake. "Roger that," he said.

"Oh, one other thing," Blake said. "Quarantine."

"Other? You already mentioned it," Paul said. "We have to land on Luna before returning to Earth, to prevent cross-contamination."

"Yes, I did, but it bears repeating. And not only Earth. You're not allowed to land *here* either, if you're coming from a terraformed planet."

"But, what about traffic from Sawyer's World?"

"That horse already left the barn, when the *Vostok* landed here after landing there, and many times since." Blake sighed. "To be honest, I imagine anything on the outside of the ship wouldn't survive a week in space followed by reentry heating, and you'd notice if there were something *inside* the ship—except possibly on the landing gear.

"Regardless, those *are* the regulations. If you're coming here from anywhere but Sawyer's or Earth, you have to quarantine on Mahina Nui, our larger moon, first. If you're heading on to Earth, you can skip quarantine and just refuel there, doing your quarantine on Luna. By the way, that also applies to Taprobane. You're fine going from here to there, but if you're returning from a new terraformed world, you're not allowed to land on the planet at all. I don't know if they have refueling facilities set up on their moon yet. If not, you may have to fend for yourself. But after landing on a new planet, you cannot land on Taprobane itself."

Paul turned to look at Mary again. "Will that be a problem?" He seemed sure it wouldn't be, and was asking more for Blake's benefit, as reassurance.

She shook her head. "It's not completely unexpected. We knew we might have to refuel on a comet or ice moon in the Pavonis system, if the planet proves hostile. It's more of a hassle, but we can deal with it."

"*Bien.*" He turned back to Blake. "Do you have any other surprises?"

"I don't," Blake said. "Although I'm sure you will find more than enough of your own. *Bonne chance.*" He rose to signal that the meeting was over.

"*Oui,*" Paul said, shaking Blake's proffered hand. "*Merci.*"

∞ ∞ ∞

Rick was waiting for them when they left Blake's office. They quickly filled him in, especially about the intelligent natives on Taprobane.

"Well, that's an unexpected twist," he said.

"It is that," agreed Paul, "but I don't see that it changes anything. Our contract with Skrellan Pharmaceuticals requires us to follow the quarantine regulations, not that we wouldn't anyway, and I'd just as soon not get distracted by a first contact situation with the Taprobane natives. As long as we can refuel there on the way out, the project proceeds as normal."

"Agreed," Mary said, "although I'm curious as to what they look like. The timoans, that is."

Paul shook his head. "We may need to send down a drone to scout a landing area. Perhaps we can spot some that way. But that's as close as we get."

"Spoilsport," Mary said.

"I would have thought you'd be a bit more sensitive about indigenous peoples being disrupted by contact with technologically advanced outsiders."

"Are you kidding?" she said. "Living on fish and blubber while hunting on foot with spears, versus modern food, snow machines, and rifles? Bring on the technologically advanced outsiders, say I. Besides, I'm only half Inuit."

Paul laughed. "All right. But we're still not going anywhere near the Taprobane natives."

Rick, who had been quiet since learning of the timoans, chose that moment to speak up.

"What are we going to do," he asked, "if Delta Pavonis has intelligent natives?"

That caught Paul short. The notion hadn't occurred to him. "That has to be extremely unlikely, surely?"

"Is it? That was the assumption up until a few years ago. Then stone artifacts were discovered on Sawyer's World, and now these iron-age aliens on Taprobane. To say nothing of the very fact that these worlds were *terraformed*. I wonder if intelligent life is more common than we thought, and maybe there's a reason for it."

"The stone-agers on Sawyer's World are long gone," Mary said. "And neither Kakuloa nor the planet at Epsilon Eridani have shown any signs of intelligent life. The spectral scans of our target planet didn't show any signs of industrial activity, did they?" Certain atmospheric pollutants could be an indicator of civilization.

"No, but—"

"Then we have nothing to worry about. Worst case, if there are inhabitants, we land somewhere remotely and don't make contact."

"If it *is* inhabited," Paul said, "that could call into question any licensing arrangements. It's a risk, but I think a very small one. We will play it as it comes."

∞ ∞ ∞

Krechet's Landing Spaceport

The *Jules Verne*'s tanks were topped up, the crew members were aboard, and everything had been secured for liftoff. The timing wasn't critical; unlike Earth, Kakuloa had little space traffic to affect a launch window, and interstellar warp travel was more a matter of being able to see the target than precisely-timed minimum-energy orbits. They were waiting on clearance from Traffic Control; a matter of making sure the field was empty and ensuring any aircraft stayed at a safe distance.

"You know," Rick said, "this is something of a historic launch."

"Why? Aside from the fact that we're headed out on what we hope is a mission of discovery," Paul said.

"This is only the second time an Anderson class starship has ever lifted from the surface of an alien planet, if you don't count the Moon."

"What? But the original Centauri Expedition had five ships," Mary protested.

"Think about it. Two of those weren't designed to land anyway, and one of them never made it into the system. Of the three landers, the *Krechet* is still out there on the field—" he waved in its general direction "—and the *Anderson* only landed on what's now Sawyer's World and is still there. Only the *Chandrasekhar* had the ability to refuel and launch."

"He's right," Paul agreed. "And after we refuel on Taprobane, we'll be the only such ship to have launched from *two* alien planets. Perhaps three, by the time we leave Delta Pavonis."

"Okay," Mary said, "but that only gets us an asterisked entry in the record books. The first ship of any class to do that was a V-class, probably the *Vostok* for two planets, maybe the *Vanguard* for three, even four."

Just then the call came in from Traffic Control. "Jules Verne, *this is Kakuloa Control. You have a fifteen-minute window coming up in ten minutes. Proceed with pre-launch prep but await final clearance.*"

"Kakuloa, copy that. *Verne* will begin pressurization and engine-chill in five. Standing by for final clearance." Mary clicked off then switched to the ship's internal speakers.

"All hands, we have preliminary clearance, T-minus nine minutes. Secure for launch. Sequencing starts in four minutes."

Unlike the newer V-class ships, the Verne's chemical ground-to-space engines still required the propellant tanks to be brought up to flight pressure to feed the turbopumps, and the pumps and engines themselves to be cooled down to avoid thermal shock from the inrush of cryogenic liquids at ignition. The former meant closing the vent valves and letting normal boil off build up tank pressure. Then a dribble of ultra-cold fuel would be bled into the engines to pre-chill them.

The computer took care of most of this, with Mary monitoring the control board while Rick double-checked that their guidance and navigation system contained the latest data from Kakuloa Control.

∞ ∞ ∞

At T-minus five minutes, they heard the vent valves close, and the background chuffing of vented gas went quiet. "Tank pressurization initiated," Mary announced.

She eyed the rise in tank pressure as the count ticked down. She keyed her microphone.

"Kakuloa, this is *Jules Verne*. Still standing by for final clearance to launch."

"*Roger that,* Verne. *Aircraft is on final approach. We'll let you know when it's clear of the field.*"

"Copy that. *Verne* will initiate auto-hold at T-minus one if nothing heard." The tanks could sit at flight pressure for a while, but other items in the launch sequence had to follow in rapid succession from the T-one mark. They could abort right up until ignition, but it would mean recycling the count from an earlier point. If it came to that, they could technically abort even after liftoff, hovering to burn fuel, and then coming back to a regular vertical landing, but nobody wanted that.

"*Understood.*"

Mary tapped the controls to tell the computer to hold at T-minus one. She'd override that as soon as ground control gave her the okay.

"Okay, crew," she announced. "We've got a slowpoke landing on the field. It's T-minus two minutes now. We'll hold at T-minus one until we get the all-clear."

Rick, beside her, grumbled something about "dang it, let's go already." He never had been good at waiting in anticipation.

∞ ∞ ∞

They watched the clock click down to T-00:01:00, then stop. A mechanical voice announced, "HOLD INITIATED."

In a calm voice that surely belied his feelings, Paul asked, "Any word on that aircraft?"

Mary had been listening to the radio traffic through her headset. "It's just touched down. We should get a *go* as soon as it's taxied clear."

"It'll probably get a flat tire on the way," Rick muttered.

Paul chuckled. "Be careful what you say. Don't give the Fates any ideas."

Any response from Rick was drowned out by the radio speaker announcing, "*Jules Verne, this is Kakuloa. You are GO for vertical departure on requested track. Report clearing atmosphere.*"

"Thank you, Kakuloa," Mary responded. "Resuming countdown from T-minus one minute at my mark." She reached a hand over the control. "Mark," she said, and tapped it. A second later, the clock ticked over to T-00:00:59, and the clicks and vents of pre-chill sequence started up again.

Two minutes after that, they were passing through Max-Q on their way to space.

Chapter 14: Epsilon Indi

Epsilon Indi star system

"Coming out of warp in three, two, one, now," Mary announced, watching the countdown timer, one hand ready at the cutoff switch.

As at Alpha Centauri, because the *Jules Verne* did not have the asymmetrical warp pod configuration and tuning necessary for artificial gravity, there was little noticeable change when the warp field cut off, except for the star showing a small, intensely bright disk out the forward windows.

"We're here," Mary said. "Stand by for maneuvers while I figure out exactly where 'here' is."

The technique for finding their position in a planetary system was a combination of ancient geometry and modern warp travel. Mary began by taking images of the star field surrounding the ship. She would then warp a couple of AUs to a different spot and repeat. Comparing the two sets of images would show the local planets as having moved relative to the fixed background of the distant stars. Given that information, she would rotate the ship to take exact sightings. Even without a published ephemeris to compare with, it was simple geometry to triangulate their position relative to their destination.

∞ ∞ ∞

An hour and several short warp transitions later, they were in high orbit above the third planet from Epsilon Indi, a star much like Kakuloa's Alpha Centauri B.

"It has very large polar caps," Paul observed. "With a name like Taprobane, I thought it would be warmer."

"Oh?"

"It's an old name for the island of Sri Lanka."

"Near India? Someone has a perverse sense of humor."

"*C'est ça*," Paul said, smiling. "I approve."

"We're getting a signal," Mary said.

"That must be the beacon that Blake mentioned," said Paul. "Put it on speaker."

"*. . . all ships. This planet is off-limits to vessels not on official UDT business. If you must land to refuel, only the following locations are authorized*"— there followed a list of coordinates, relative to a beacon in synchronous orbit, then the message began to repeat.

"Did you get those?" Paul asked.

"Copied," Mary said. "Now, let's see if any of them have nice weather."

∞ ∞ ∞

Two of the three designated landing sites did have acceptable weather, and one of them was even in daylight. All were on islands.

"I think they were serious about not having any contact with the natives," Rick said as they discussed this. "I take it the timoans aren't particularly seafaring."

"Probably not," Paul said, "but there's nothing in the information we received that says one way or the other."

"I have to wonder how far the nearest settlements are. Do you suppose having a ship land or lift generates a UFO report?"

"Who would they report it to? 'I saw a strange light in the sky and heard a booming sound.' That could just be thunder and lightning to a primitive," said Mary. "But I'm sure the sites were carefully picked to be away from any obvious villages. They certainly weren't picked for convenience of landing."

"They look boring," Kristen said as they scanned the sites from low orbit. "Flat islands, enough above water so that they're not swamped, but no interesting geology. They don't have much in the way of vegetation, from the looks of it."

"Which means not much in the way of animals, either," Corey observed.

"That's probably the idea," said Paul. "They don't want people hanging around. I imagine the nearest natives are hundreds if not thousands of kilometers away."

"Boring is good," Mary said. "If we're landing on an unprepared field, boring is very good. I just wish there was more land around them."

"Worried you won't hit your target?" Paul asked lightly.

Mary gave him a dirty look. "I could do that even without the beacon. But I like a margin in case of unexpected winds or something. Presumably, the site has already been checked out, at least. We won't have that luxury where we're going next."

"Good point. But they probably had V-class ships in mind when they picked the sites, not something like the *Jules Verne*. Will it make a difference?"

"We should be fine. If anything, we have a smaller landing footprint. We can't tolerate as much deviation from horizontal on the landing surface, but this site looks good."

"*Bien*. Get us ready for EDL,—" entry, descent, and landing "—and let's go tank up."

∞ ∞ ∞

On Taprobane's surface

The entry to landing sequence went as routinely as it had on Kakuloa, and in less than twenty minutes the *Jules Verne* had set down on a clear plain near a low cliff overlooking the sea.

Like the Mediterranean on Earth, this sea connected to the larger world ocean by a series of straights. This geography reduced the chances of rough sea weather near the landing site. For refueling the fusion plant, seawater was preferable to freshwater for its enrichment in deuterium. (The hydrogen- and methane-burning rocket engines, which would lift the *Verne* back to orbit, didn't care what kind of hydrogen they burned, light or heavy, although the former gave better performance.)

"We seem to be a long way from the water," Paul observed. It looked like they were forty meters from the cliff edge.

"There's no GPS here, only a beacon," Mary said, "I didn't want to get too close to the edge. Especially since I don't know how solid it is."

"All right, but do we have enough hose to reach that?"

"Fortunately, we only need enough high-pressure hose to pump the water up the cliff," Rick said. Because the plain they were on was less than ten meters above the water line, the needed pressure wouldn't be very high. "The rest of it is low-pressure hose that rolls up a lot tighter. We have plenty."

"Okay then. Atmosphere check first."

"Why?" Corey asked. "We know it's terraformed, and people have landed here before." In fact, they had seen evidence of scorch marks from another ship's jets as they approached.

"We can use the practice, and perhaps something changed recently."

Corey sighed. "Aye, aye, Captain."

∞ ∞ ∞

Taprobane fueling station #2

Refueling the *Jules Verne* here was more complicated than fueling on Earth or, for that matter, Kakuloa, had been. It held one surprise, but a pleasant one.

The atmosphere checked out, of course, and Rick and Corey made ready to exit the ship.

"Do we need to wear the BIGs?" Rick asked. "This place has been checked out already, right?" The BIGs—Biological Isolation Garments—were standard kit for the first few days on a new planet. They would prevent contamination in either direction until testing had demonstrated that it was unlikely.

"No," Paul said, "the information we have has cleared the planet for that. Although it might be good practice."

Rick started to object, then caught Paul's grin. "Right. I'll pass on that. I won't be going out first at our next stop anyway."

"True, that. But you might want to bundle up. It's kind of cool out there. Only ten degrees Celsius."

"But we're near the equator!"

"We're south of it, and it's southern hemisphere winter. And maybe this island is in the middle of a cold current."

"Okay," Rick said, taking a jacket from one of the mid-deck storage lockers. He also grabbed a pair of waterproof work gloves. Corey did likewise.

With the two of them bundled up, they stepped into the air-lock and sealed the inner door behind them.

"Opening the outer door now," Rick reported.

"Make sure your safety lines are secured. I don't want either of you falling out; it's a long drop."

"Roger that." Rick and Corey double-checked each other's safety lines, hooked to harnesses at one end, with the other feed-ing from automatic winches anchored to the bulkhead. The winches would pay out as they descended the ladder, taking most of their weight to help their zero-gee weakened muscles cope. Their reels would lock automatically if they started to fall, and could help winch them up on return.

"Okay, Rick said, "stepping out now."

Getting down on hands and knees, Rick backed out over the rim of the airlock hatch, groping around with one foot until he found the ladder rung. He tested his footing, then brought his other leg down to stand on the top rung, his hands still gripping the handrail mounted inside the hatch.

He looked around, taking in the scenery. The island they were on was mostly rock, but there were outcrops of vegetation higher up from the landing area. The landing area itself looked as though it had been, at least partially, carved out of the rock and artificially leveled. Probably Space Force's doing, given that this was a desig-nated landing area. He turned to look out to sea. Aside from a few rocks perhaps fifty meters offshore, he could see nothing but water, with low waves rolling in.

From the open hatchway, Corey had been looking out too. "We must be a long way from any mainland," he said. "On Earth, a rock like this would be covered with seabirds."

"Do they even have birds on this planet?"

"I'd be very surprised if they didn't. Kakuloa and Sawyer's World have birds, so does Spitzer. They're an important part of the ecosystem."

"Maybe along with the beacon, the Space Force set up something to keep them away."

"That's possible," Corey said. "They do that at some airports. But I don't see any guano deposits either. There haven't been birds here for a long time, if ever."

"Well, it's not our problem. We're just here to refuel." By now, Rick had reached the bottom of the ladder. He stepped off and looked around. He was hardly the first human to set foot here, so he unhooked his line and simply said, "I'm off the ladder. Corey, come on down."

"On my way."

As Corey made his way down, Rick took a few steps back and gave the *Verne* a visual once over. "The ship looks fine," he said. "Nice landing."

"*Thanks. Any time.*" Mary's voice came back over his headset.

Rick surveyed the landing zone. It had definitely been artificially leveled, he decided. There were scrape marks on the rock, and places where it looked like cracks had been filled in. *I wonder*, he thought, *if they did anything to make refueling easier?* It would certainly make his job simpler. He moved to look over the edge of the bluff. It overlooked a narrow beach, and there seemed to be an easy climb down and back. The problem would be extending their intake hose out far enough to avoid getting sand sucked into it. Maybe they could rig up a buoy.

As Rick turned to check on Corey, he caught sight of an odd-looking boulder at the edge of the bluff. At a meter high and a bit more than that wide, it looked far too regular to be natural. He went over and examined it, then banged at it, producing a hollow-sounding *THUNK*. He looked at it more closely and found a seam in the artificial rock face.

"What are you playing with rocks for?" came Corey's voice from behind him. "We're supposed to be getting the hoses out."

Rick turned and grinned at him. "Look what I found!" He turned back to the 'rock' and pulled up at the seam. The lid opened, revealing several hose couplings, valves, and a power connector. "Somebody very kindly set us up with plumbing down into the sea." He cautiously leaned over the edge of the bluff beside the artificial boulder and, sure enough, could make out a set of pipes running down from it into the water. They had been painted to match the rock surface.

"Very handy indeed," Corey agreed. "I guess the *UDT* doesn't want anyone spending any more time here than they have to."

"Makes sense. Nobody told us about these, though. Must be new." Since they'd been deliberately camouflaged, their age was difficult to tell. The fittings in the box, though, were still shiny. No more than a month or two, Rick decided. He chuckled. At Corey's quizzical look, he said, "I have to wonder what any natives who stumbled across this would think."

"We're way out at sea. Even if they do have boats capable of coming out this far, I don't think there's anything to make this island worth visiting."

"No, probably not. Okay," he said, stepping away from the edge of the bluff, "let's get the hoses to hook this up to the ship."

The box turned out to have not only the plumbing, but also a pump, although the latter required them to run a power connection from the ship.

"If they were going to install pumps, why not install the power supply too?" Rick wondered.

Corey shrugged. "Like what? How long would batteries last? And they probably wouldn't want to leave anything too high-tech in case natives did end up finding it."

"I suppose. It's a good thing we brought extension cords."

Corey just shook his head. "First rule of camping. Always bring extension cords."

"*First* rule?"

"Okay, maybe not. But certainly up there."

∞ ∞ ∞

As Rick had said, they had plenty of low-pressure hose to run from the bluff's edge to the ship. Made from a reinforced polymer film, it lay flat when unrolled, more like a long, thin, plastic bag than a fuel hose. That was fine. It carried water, not cryogens, and didn't have to stand up to much wear or pressure.

One of the modifications made during the refit of the *Verne* had been to include a more compact version of the electrolysis and cryo-cooling systems that, on the original Alpha Centauri expedition, had been contained in the separate refueling module, together with its nuclear fission reactor and shielding. The *Verne*'s compact fusion unit sidestepped the need for all that.

The refueling process would take the better part of two days. The *Verne*'s gear extracted needed deuterium from water. A standard ion-exchange system filtered out the salt and returned it to the ocean, then the deuterium component—heavy water—was separated out for electrolysis, splitting the remaining freshwater into oxygen and hydrogen. Some of the hydrogen was then reacted with carbon dioxide from the air to produce methane, in a process as old as the first manned Mars expeditions. Most of this was to fuel the chemical rocket engines so they could boost back to space, saving the deuterium to fuel the warp drive.

The onboard fusion unit supplied the energy for all this, with a tiny portion of the extracted deuterium siphoned off to fuel it. Excess heat was pumped back into the ocean along with the more-concentrated brine.

By the second day, the layer of warmed water near the landing site had begun to form a low fog bank.

"That adds to the mystery of the island," Rick observed when Corey remarked on it. "It's almost a pity there aren't any natives near enough to see it. Think of the stories they'd come up with."

"It won't last. It will dissipate when the wind picks up, or with a change in the currents. Maybe even with the tide. Was it there last night?"

"It was dark. Who could tell?"

∞ ∞ ∞

"Well, I'm very disappointed in this truck stop," Rick said late on the second day. "The scenery is boring, the restrooms are non-existent, and there's no food or coffee but what we have in the ship. One star."

"At least there's fuel," Mary chided. "What were you expecting, a Tim Horton's?"

"*Tim Horton's!* Man, I could go for a donut right now. Is that something in the autochef's repertoire?"

"Something almost, but not quite, completely unlike donuts, maybe, but certainly nothing up to Tim Horton standards."

"What's special about Tim Horton's?" Kristen asked. "Are they like Krispy Kreme donuts?"

"More like Dunkin' Donuts," Rick said. "Coffee and other food too."

"It's a Canadian thing," Paul explained. "You wouldn't understand." Kristen was American. "I've lived in Canada for three years, and *I* don't understand—but then I'm French. Donuts are an abomination." He grinned at the outraged expression on Rick's face. "Give me *cannelés* . . . or even an éclair."

"Well, at least we have coffee." Rick said.

∞ ∞ ∞

"Okay, people, the *Verne* is almost fully fueled. Check that everything is stowed for launch. Last chance for fresh air for another two weeks," Paul roused the crew.

"That's if the planet at Delta Pavonis is terraformed," Rick pointed out. "Otherwise, it will be a month before we're back here—assuming we have a way to fuel up when we get there."

"Do you want to wait for us here? I suppose we could leave you with food and a tent. But no donuts, sorry."

Rick glared at him. "You know that's not what I meant. And I'm not worried. We've been over contingencies for fueling from an ice moon or comet body. I'll be very surprised if the Delta Pavonis system doesn't have both."

"Relax, my friend. I didn't think you did. But it is worth bringing up. From here on, we are going into literally unexplored territory. I don't want to force anyone, so, last chance to back out."

"Are you kidding?" Rick said. "I wouldn't miss this for the world."

"You're not going anywhere without a pilot," Mary said.

"The ship can virtually fly itself," Paul said. "And I am a pilot." He didn't have near the number of hours behind the controls of a plane that Mary had, but the *Verne* wasn't a plane, was fully automated, and he'd taken space pilot training right alongside her.

She grinned at him. "Let me rephrase that. You're not going anywhere without *this* pilot," she pointed a thumb at her chest. "I'm coming with you."

"Ah, *bien*."

"Likewise," Corey said. "If there's biology there, I want in. If there's not, well, I'm still getting paid, right?" He smiled at that last.

"Yes," Paul agreed. "Just not as much."

Corey shrugged. "There's oxygen in the atmosphere. There's life."

"Kristen?"

"Why are we standing around gabbing when we need to finish loading the ship? Of *course* I'm going. I already said this place was boring, didn't I?"

Paul nodded, smiling. "*Oui*. Let's get to it then."

The others dispersed to their tasks, except for Rick.

"What about the refueling gear?" he asked Paul.

"We'll stow that last, to keep the tanks as topped up as possible. And purge the seawater lines with steam before stowing them. We don't want crud growing in them while we're in transit, and we don't want to transplant anything from the ocean here to Delta Pavonis."

"Copy that."

A short while later, the gear had been stowed, including the fueling lines. The faux boulder hiding the hose couplings had been restored to its original closed condition, and the landing field patrolled for anything loose that the ship's exhaust might kick up.

Paul and Mary did a final walk-around, then clipped into the safety lines for the ladder. Mary went up first, the reel taking up most of her weight. Then, with a final look around, Paul followed. He paused at the airlock door to retract the ladder, then with an "*au revoir, Taprobane*," he closed and secured the hatch. "All right," he said as he left the airlock for the main cabin, "prepare for take-off."

∞ ∞ ∞

Aboard Jules Verne

"How are we looking, Mary?" Paul asked.

"Everything's green on the board. We're go for launch."

"Winds aloft?"

"Laser and doppler say within tolerance. Actually, we have plenty of margin."

"Good. How's our timing?" It shouldn't be critical, they didn't have a rendezvous to make, but it would be nice to make it to space with a clear shot at their destination without having to wait in orbit.

"Delta Pavonis is above the horizon in six minutes at my mark . . . and, mark."

"Roger that." Paul clicked on the PA system. "All hands, T minus six minutes. We're go for launch."

The next six minutes were interminable. This wasn't like the takeoff from French Guiana, where the ship had been interfaced with ground support equipment up until the last few seconds, or even Kakuloa, where a fuel truck had stood by keeping their tanks topped up against boil-off, and they had been chatting with Space Traffic Control. Mary's job here was limited to watching the computer watch the ship's systems, and occasionally calling out their progress. The latter was as much to keep everyone else entertained as informed; there wasn't anything they could do with the information.

"Valves shut, tanks coming to flight pressure," she said, and continued with periodic updates.

"T minus seventy, going to automatic in ten."

"T minus thirty, engine pre-chill commencing. Everything is still green, looks like a go."

"Confirm GO for launch," Paul said.

"Roger GO. T minus ten seconds."

From below came the sounds of valves opening and turbines spooling up. "Ignition sequence start"

The sounds from below rose to a deafening, rushing roar, the vibrations surging through the ship. Then they were all pressed back into their couches.

"And we have liftoff!" Mary shouted above the roar.

Eight minutes later, they were in orbit above the blue-white surface of Taprobane.

And then they were on their way to Delta Pavonis and whatever mysteries its green planet held.

Chapter 15: *Matthew* at Kakuloa

Kakuloa, Alpha Centauri System

"What do you have for me today, Gene?" Blake asked his aide upon entering his office. A mug of hot coffee already awaited him on his desk.

"Good morning, sir. Monthly production reports from Bimini Mines, request to expand squid-tree cultivation from Manning and some of the farms to the north, an exploration report from the Orellana expedition, and the *Matthew* has just reported entering the system. Due to land at eleven-hundred." He swiped his pad to copy the files to Blake's desktop.

Blake took a long drink of his coffee. It was going to be one of those days. Wait, the *Matthew*? "Edward Talbot's ship? I thought the *Matthew* was going to be laid up for several months for maintenance. It was just here a couple of weeks ago."

"That's correct. Apparently, a change of plans. Shall I have the captain report to you when they land?"

That wouldn't normally be necessary. Blake liked to greet the captains of ships that hadn't visited Kakuloa before, but that was more courtesy and his own curiosity than any official requirement. The *Matthew* had a routine light cargo run between Earth and Alpha Centauri, and he had met Talbot before.

"No, not for a routine visit." He gestured at the file icons on his desktop. "I have enough to keep me busy."

∞ ∞ ∞

Aboard the Matthew

"We're cleared for EDL, Captain. Five minutes to entry burn," the *Matthew*'s pilot reported.

"Copy that," Talbot said and made the announcement to the ship's crew, and his two scientist passengers.

"Now listen up," he added. "We're running behind schedule, and we have minimal cargo to unload here—" just enough for their cover story "—so this will be a short stay. No shore leave. There'll be plenty of that when we get to where we're going. About that, mum's the word. We don't want details leaking out. Now, secure for landing."

A half-hour later, the *Matthew* sat cooling on the parking apron at the Krechet's Landing spaceport.

∞ ∞ ∞

Krechet's Landing

Talbot strolled into the spaceport cargo office with a datapad under his arm. The ship's manifest, or at least what was being unloaded here, and the data on the ship's complement was already in the computers, having been transmitted from orbit. This visit, like the datapad, was mostly a formality, and partly a tradition.

"Captain Talbot," the freight agent, Pete Kanigowski, said. "We weren't expecting to see you back so soon. Repairs on the *Matthew* all complete, then?"

"The important ones, anyway. Slight change of plans, thanks to my bosses. They tell me to fly, and so long as the ship's spaceworthy, I fly." He handed the pad across to Kanigowski.

"I hear you. Let's see what you have." He glanced at the pad, then cross-checked against a readout on his desk screen. "Oh. You're traveling light this time?"

"Yes, just a few crates. The XO is already unloading them. You're not my only stop this trip."

"Ah, then I guess that would explain the two passengers. Where to next? Sawyer's World?"

"A bit farther than that. We're delivering a couple of scientists to a new world." Talbot said, smiling as if to say, *I'd like to tell you, but I can't.*

The agent frowned briefly. "Well, Epsilon Indi is off-limits, or at least the planet is. Epsilon Eridani?"

Talbot grinned. "Just a tad farther."

"Tau Ceti? I thought its world was high mass?" Word got around at the spaceport, details of new planets especially so.

Gotcha, thought Talbot. He smiled. They would actually be going to Epsilon Indi. Even if the planet were off-limits, there would be somewhere in the system to refuel. But it was better if Kanigowski thought he would be going to Tau Ceti, precisely because of how quickly spaceport gossip spread.

"It's actually a double planet," Talbot continued, "but you didn't hear that from me." Everything he'd said was literally true. Delta Pavonis *was* a bit farther than Epsilon Eridani, albeit in a slightly different direction, and the latest word was that Tau Ceti *did* turn out to have a double in its habitable zone. Some other crew could check those out.

"Ahh, hear what?" the agent said, winking.

Ed Talbot left the office, happy that he'd sidestepped Kanigowski's questions about their next destination but disappointed not to have been able to work questions about the *Jules Verne* into the conversation without arousing suspicion. No matter, he could casually ask one of the ramp rats working to refuel the *Matthew*. They would know the comings and goings of spacecraft as well as anyone.

Part III - Delta Pavonis

Chapter 16: Into the System

Deep space, aboard the Jules Verne

The *Verne* was thirty light-days from Delta Pavonis now. It had dropped out of warp for a final position check, and Mary began lining it up for the final jump to the outskirts of the system.

"I don't get it," Corey, said. "Wouldn't it be faster to just head right into the system? Why mess around in whatever passes for an Oort Cloud, or Kuiper Belt, or whatever Delta Pavonis has?"

"Because we don't want to hit something at warp speed. Remember the *Xing Hua*?"

"The Chinese ship on the first Centauri expedition? What about it?"

"It hit something in the outskirts of the system and exploded."

"Actually, no, it didn't," Rick said. "They faked the explosion, probably using a small nuke, then came back to Earth so they could reverse-engineer the warp drive. Then they went to the Epsilon Eridani system."

"You don't believe that conspiracy theory, do you? They made that up to let Commodore Drake off the hook."

"No," Mary said, "he's right. The Chinese circulated the conspiracy rumor to cover up what they'd been doing. Especially after they really did lose a ship in the Eridani system."

"But that ship didn't hit anything. It was aliens."

Several of the others made rude noises at that.

"All right, settle down, *mes amis*," Paul said. "Regardless of what may have happened, or not, to Chinese ships, we don't want anything to happen to *this* ship. It is true that after the *Xing Hua* disappearance, the rest of the expedition proceeded more cautiously into the Alpha Centauri system, and that's a clearer system than this one. Rick, why don't you explain that."

"Explain what? Oh, I get you. Yes. The Alpha Centauri system actually has a lower risk of hitting miscellaneous debris than Delta Pavonis, or for that matter, Epsilon Eridani or any other singleton star.

"The thing is," he continued, "because Alpha Centauri A and B are relatively close to each other—the distance varies as roughly the distance of Saturn to Neptune in our solar system—the gravitational interaction means that most orbits of anything between them are unstable. Anything there will eventually get kicked out into interstellar space."

"But both A and B have planets. We were on one of them a couple of weeks ago."

"They do, but only a few, and close in. It's a happy coincidence that the habitable zones of both stars lie close enough to each to be in one of the stable orbit zones. Much farther out and they'd be unstable. Although, if you get far enough out from both stars they can be treated as a single gravitational point."

"Coincidence, or Terraformers?" Corey asked.

"*Probably* coincidence," Rick said, "because the systems are billions of years old, and the terraforming was done only sixty-five or so million years ago. But who knows?

"Anyway," Rick continued, "as I was saying, most of the Centauri system is clear. When you only have one star, you might get narrow bands where orbits are unstable because of the influence of, say, a gas giant—our own system has what are called the

Kirkwood gaps in the asteroid belt because of Jupiter—but there will be a lot of other crap floating around. Like those asteroids I just mentioned. Epsilon Eridani has two asteroid belts. We haven't spotted any asteroid belt as such in the Delta Pavonis system, but that certainly doesn't mean the system is clear. It might be—the system is a billion years older than ours—but why take the chance?"

"So, we do what, creep into the system on thrusters?" Corey said. "It will take weeks to get to the planet of interest."

"No," Paul said. "We edge up to the system, look very carefully at it, then take short hops along whichever route looks emptiest—probably out of the ecliptic—and looking around carefully between them. It shouldn't take more than a day or two. Besides, that gives us more time to collect the data that the *UDT* Astronomical Survey Group is going to pay us for."

∞ ∞ ∞

Jules Verne*, entering the Delta Pavonis system*

"Coming out of warp, stand by," Mary announced. As when they had arrived at Alpha Centauri, because the warp geometry of the *Verne* did not provide any artificial gravity, there wasn't any noticeable difference when the warp field cut off. Except that they should now be able to see something on the viewers.

Sure enough, after a barely-noticed flicker of the lighting as the power to the warp drive shut off, stars became visible on the viewscreen. She dimmed the cabin lights to let them see out the windows, too.

"Well," Paul said, "there's a bright star out there. I assume that's our target. I don't see much else."

"Good, nor should you," Mary said. "The idea is to stop far enough away from the system to avoid hitting anything."

"Of course. I'm just confirming it."

They were a hundred AU from the star itself. The next step would be to photograph the area, shift a couple of AU with a small warp jump, and then rephotograph it. The background stars wouldn't move, but anything nearby would have shifted position, the greater the shift, the closer the object. They had schematics of the system based on telescopic observation mostly from Earth, and verified by observations in the Alpha Centauri system, but since nobody had visited the system yet, that was all they had. Detailed knowledge of where the other planets in the system were, including both the Jupiter-sized one and the green Earth-mass planet they were headed for, and most especially, any cometary or asteroid belts that they would be best to avoid, would take further observation and analysis. While they were doing this for their own safety, the data was of enough value to future visitors that the *UDT* had offered a contract to pay for it. The ingenuity of the Paon Company team in coming up with ways to extract profit from this trip had amazed Rick.

"My father is always telling me not to leave money on the table," Paul had explained.

"Okay," Mary reported, "first set of photos complete. Warping to the next position . . . now." The screens and windows flickered for the few seconds they were in warp, and then cleared again.

Paul, who had remained at the window, said, "I'm pretty sure we moved, but that's about all."

"We did. Commencing the next photo sweep now." Mary's fingers tapped out the commands on her panel. "We'll want to do another one after this, just to be sure."

"And then again in a few days," Paul said, "to give some time difference for calculating orbits. I remember."

"Exactly," she said.

∞ ∞ ∞

Aboard the Jules Verne

They gathered in the mid-deck to go over the data analysis.

"So, this system has at least six planets," Rick said, displaying a schematic. "It's possible there's something hiding behind Delta Pavonis from here, but it would have to be close for us not to have seen it."

He changed the image to that of a fuzzy green dot. "Our target is the third one from the star, Delta Pavonis III. It's in the habitable zone, so that confirms the observations from Earth.

The two planets closer in are both small and rocky, roughly Mercury- and Mars-sized, respectively.

"Then there's the gas giant, quite a bit farther out. It looks like it has at least a handful of moons, which is unsurprising. We'll take a closer look to get more detail and get an analysis of their makeup."

"Does the third planet have a moon?" Paul asked. A big moon was believed helpful in maintaining a planet's stability, and the five so far known Earth-like worlds all had large moons.

"It does, so that's another point in its favor. Of course, we'll know soon enough if its terraformed."

"*Bien.* Continue."

"Beyond the Jovian, let's call it Zeus for now, we have a Neptunian planet, and then a sub-Neptune as the furthest out."

"What about asteroids, plutoids, and the like?"

"There's a belt between III and IV, similar to our asteroid belt. There are smaller objects scattered some distance beyond VI, too small to get any detail on. Little more than pixels in the images, and some of them might even be noise. But most of them are in positions that would make sense for a Kuiper belt."

"That's not a lot of detail."

"It would take months doing surveys with better telescopes than we have to find everything. Well, not even everything, but the biggest stuff, anyway. Nobody is expecting us to do that. We only need some representative samples to get an idea of the isotope distribution in the system."

"Why do we need that?" Corey Ogden asked.

"It tells us something about the history of the system. Isotope ratios tend to vary by distance from the star, due to differentiation of the protoplanetary nebula when the system formed." Rick paused and grinned. "But to really answer your question, because the *UDT* Astronomical Survey Group is paying us to collect the data."

"All right." Paul said, bringing the discussion back on track. "What about our path inwards?"

"We'll head up north of the ecliptic, well out of the plane of rotation," Mary said. "That should avoid almost everything. There's still a chance of something in an oddball orbit, but we've identified the dust trails from a dozen long-period comets. We'll stay well clear of them."

"*Bien*. Fair enough." Paul looked at each of his team. "Everyone comfortable with this? The risk is no worse than flying out of our own solar system, or what we did in the Epsilon Indi system." He looked at Rick and Mary. "Is that a fair statement?"

"As near as we can figure. The computer models concur," Rick said.

"If you guys are comfortable with it," Corey said, "I'm good. If we do hit something, we'll never know it, right?"

Rick nodded. "Most likely, but we won't."

Kristen said, "Sure. It can't be any riskier than flying a helicopter into the mountains. Let's go. Ice moons and gas giants are boring. I want to see why that planet is green." Their initial telescopic observation hadn't shown much more detail than the few-pixel green dot from the fifty-meter telescope back in the Sol system. It still showed as a round blob, but with more pixels of various shades of green, and a hint of white at the poles.

"Maybe it's a swamp world, like old Venus," Mary said.

Rick looked at her in disbelief. "*Venus*? Are you kidding me?"

"I meant the wet Venus of old science fiction, of course," she said. At his skeptical look, she added, "Both Robert Heinlein and Poul Anderson, before the early interplanetary probes showed differently, wrote stories set on a Venus covered in swamps and jungles."

"True," Rick allowed, "but you'd think they'd have known better."

"It was a common trope," Paul said. "Some of the early *Perry Rhodan* stories had that too, as did others. I remember one, not a Rhodan, but by Ray Bradbury, where it was raining all the time."

"But if it were raining all the time," Mary said, "all we would see from space is cloud tops. It would look white, not green." She'd flown above enough rain clouds to know.

"We may see more white when we get closer," Rick said. "At this distance, we can't see much, even with the onboard telescope."

"All right then, let's get closer." Paul looked around at his crew, then, to Mary, said, "Next stop, somewhere near the third planet, right?"

"Not quite," she said. "We can't make a turn in warp, and we want a clear path, so next stop is somewhere north of the ecliptic. But then, Delta Pavonis III, yes."

"Very good." Paul grinned. "Make it so."

Chapter 17: Approaching the Target

Approaching Delta Pavonis III

"How soon will we be able to land?" Paul asked, eager to get on the ground.

"We need to find a landing site first," Mary said, "but—"

"How long will that take?"

"—but even then, we need a precise measurement of this planet's gravity and its atmospheric pressure gradient. We already knew those at Kakuloa and Taprobane."

Paul knew she was right. Their entry, descent and landing profile would depend on that data, and getting it wrong could mean an entry too steep for their heat shield or lead them to a hard landing, either burning too late or running out of landing fuel too soon.

"We can get that while surveying for landing sites, can't we?"

"Yes," Rick said. "We just need a rough orbit at first. Once I get some observations, I can refine the data while the rest of you pick out some likely landing areas. We'll follow the original Alpha Centauri expedition procedures."

"And how long will it take?"

"A couple of days?"

"That long?"

"What were you expecting? 'Enter standard orbit and prepare an away team?'" Rick grinned. "It doesn't work like that. The newer V-class ships have more flexibility, but it still takes many orbits to build up good maps."

Paul sighed. "*D'accord.* You're right. Carry on."

∞ ∞ ∞

Delta Pavonis system

The data they had collected so far comprised telescopic observations of all the planets from several points as they had made their way into the system. The outer two Neptune-like objects weren't very different from Uranus or Neptune in the Solar system, although one was much smaller. They had several small moons, little more than icy asteroids.

The gas giant, Zeus, was more interesting, with colorful banding much like Jupiter, or the gas giant Aegir in the Epsilon Eridani system. It had a thin ring system, much less spectacular than Saturn's, but bigger than Jupiter's. They had spotted three moons large enough to be spherical, roughly the size of Jupiter's Galilean moons, with one of them icy like Europa. It orbited far enough out from the planet that it was clear of most of the Van Allen-like radiation fields typical of a gas giant, so could serve as a refueling spot in a pinch. The *Verne*'s systems worked best with liquid water, but ice could be managed. They could melt even the granite-hard ice of a moon in the outer system.

The third planet, the one they now orbited, had a single large moon, as they had observed as they approached the system. Slightly smaller but denser than Earth's own moon, it lacked the large maria or basalt "seas" of the latter. In that respect, it more resembled Mahina Nui orbiting Kakuloa, or Selene orbiting Sawyer's World, although it did have an odd random pattern of streaks and spots of darker material against the generally light-colored surface. In fact, the surface was no paler than the dark grey of the Earth's Moon, it just looked so against the black sky. However, the mottled pattern of darker mountain peaks and ridges gave the body a distinctive appearance.

To Paul, it reminded him of a kind of blue cheese from his native Jura region of France, *Bleu de Gex*, and in the spirit of the amusing Anglophone legend that Earth's Moon was made of cheese, he so named this moon. At the protests of the rest of the crew, he allowed it to be shortened to *Gex*, not that that did much to mollify them.

Given the appearance of the planet beneath them, he had an idea for its name too, but that would wait until he set foot on it.

"Do we have enough data for landing calculations?" he asked Rick.

"Mostly. The surface gravity is slightly less than Earth's, but the atmosphere is thicker. That helps us on the way down, but will hinder us during ascent. Mary and I are still crunching numbers on the best flight profiles."

"And the air is breathable?"

"So far I haven't seen any reason why not. It has more oxygen and argon than Earth's air. As a percentage, there's slightly less nitrogen, although with the thicker air, the partial pressure is higher. None of that should be a problem, unless we were going scuba diving, which we're not." They hadn't brought the gear. It was the sort of thing that could wait for a follow-up expedition, if it looked worthwhile.

"So that's a 'yes, it is breathable?'"

"We need to do more mapping orbits anyway," Rick said, refusing to be pinned down. "I'll use the time to screen for anything that could be harmful even at low levels. Because this planet is denser than Earth, I particularly want to check the radon levels."

That made sense to Paul. The higher density could mean more uranium in the rocks. The parent star had more heavy elements than Earth's sun, after all. "Very well. Keep me posted."

∞ ∞ ∞

Above Delta Pavonis III

The *Jules Verne* circled the planet in a high-inclination orbit, sweeping nearly from pole to pole to get the maximum coverage for its orbital scans. While the body below them was largely, almost overwhelmingly, green, there was some variation. Both poles had ice caps, and the skies above them were largely clear. The southern pole was water-covered, or would be if the sea ice melted in its summer. Massive glaciers covered the landlocked north pole, with a mountain range poking up through the thick ice.

Elsewhere, the ground was largely hidden by clouds streaked in various shades of green, like a pale malachite, and even the ocean showed more green than blue. Here and there, a white frosting of high-altitude cloud accented the green monotony. Where the cloud cover thinned or disappeared altogether, it revealed the darker green of forest, or occasionally the tawny brown of a desert.

"The oxygen content is twenty-five percent, but I don't understand why it isn't even higher than that," Rick said, examining the readings on the atmosphere. "All this green, it has to be plants. They must be photosynthesizing like crazy."

"Plants consume oxygen too," Corey, the biologist, said. "Maybe photosynthesis here isn't as efficient as we've found elsewhere. It will be interesting to compare."

"It would be the same chlorophyll, wouldn't it?" asked Paul, suddenly concerned. "If it isn't, would that mean this planet isn't terraformed, and it evolved life independently?"

"Wouldn't that be even better than terraformed? But no, not necessarily. It could be that this sun doesn't put out the optimum frequencies for Terran life, although sixty-million years should be enough to evolve to adapt. Or maybe there's something else in the soil or atmosphere that inhibits it."

"Or it could be that we're seeing it at a different stage of dynamic equilibrium," the geologist, Kristen, said.

"What do you mean?"

"The oxygen content of Earth's atmosphere has varied by quite a bit over its history. Millions of years ago, it was even higher than here. But what I meant was, as oxygen levels in the air increase, everything becomes more flammable. There are more wildfires. They both consume the oxygen and kill the vegetation, so O_2 levels start to drop, reducing the fire risk. It also depends on the CO_2 levels. Less CO_2 in the air, the less oxygen plants can produce. What's the carbon-dioxide level?"

"Only about 230 parts per million," Rick told her.

"That's low, although not quite as low as during Earth's ice ages. Perhaps something else is locking up the CO_2."

"But plants actually produce oxygen from water," Corey objected. "They split the H_2O to oxygen and hydrogen, then combine the hydrogen with CO_2 to make carbohydrates."

"Sure," she agreed, "but CO_2 is still the limiting reactant. There's plenty of water."

"That would also limit the growth of the plants," Rick said, "which doesn't seem to be a problem here."

"It's possible the planet is coming out of a recent ice age, or about to go into one. We'll just have to land and investigate further. I doubt we'll solve it, though—we're still trying to figure out all the details of Kakuloa and Sawyer's World ecology and climate. Best we can do is gather all the data we can."

"And that's part of what we're getting paid for," Paul reminded them. "Although if you can publish scientific papers explaining what we find, more power to you."

"And more prestige to the company," Mary added.

"Yes, that too," Paul said, "but prestige alone doesn't pay the bills." He turned back to the others. "Have you determined what all that green actually is?"

"Our best guess is some kind of airborne algae, like pond scum only small and light enough to drift on the winds," Corey said.

"Does that mean the winds are strong? Will that be a problem with entry, descent, and landing?"

Rick shook his head. "We're not seeing any indication of that in the cloud patterns. When we finish the ground scans, we'll switch to Doppler radar and get better measurements of the wind speeds."

"Have the scans turned up anywhere to land? We don't want to land in the desert; we have to collect biological samples for Skrellan."

"Yes, the rest of it isn't all jungle. There are several clear areas, even aside from the deserts. We might want to wait until the airborne weed above one is thinner."

"Would it be dangerous to descend through it?" he looked at Mary.

"I don't think so," she said. "But we want to drop a drone first anyway; that will tell us more."

"Okay, we'll do that after the Doppler scans. How long?"

"Another thirty orbits, or two days for full coverage. If we change our orbit track to skip the poles, maybe half that, but complete coverage is worth more."

Paul considered this. They had several sub-satellites they could deploy for continued data collection while they were on the surface, but they lacked the resolution of the larger, higher-powered radars on the ship. Paul also had a time limit; they wanted to be back on Earth by start of fall semester, and they would spend some time on the Moon in quarantine before that. Another day in orbit for better atmospheric data, or another day on the surface collection biological and geological specimens? It was an easy decision.

"We'll use one of the sub-satellites to complete the Doppler radar survey. We land as soon as we can find a thin patch of weed over a good touchdown spot. Get ready to deploy a drone over the most likely area."

"Define, 'most likely area,'" Rick said.

"You can figure that out between yourselves. For the Centauri expedition, it was a combination of accessibility, proximity to different ecosystems, and source of water to generate fuel. I don't see any reason to change those criteria, but if you do, I'm willing to listen. Okay?"

"Sure. What are you going to do?"

"Captain stuff. I need to go over the data we've collected so far and begin outlining report summaries, review our consumables usage, things like that. Plan our stay."

"Geez, that sounds like work," Rick said.

"I'm sorry, did you think this was going to be a vacation?"

∞ ∞ ∞

Aboard Jules Verne*, in orbit*

"Can you summarize the data we have for the planet below us?" Paul asked his team. "What are we going to be looking at when we land?"

"I'll give you the basic orbital parameters first," Rick said. "The planet has a pretty circular orbit, with an average distance of 165,306,000 kilometers from the sun, Delta Pavonis."

"Distance from the surface or the center?" Paul asked.

"From the center. I guess I should have said average orbital radius. That's 1.105 astronomical units. I calculate the orbital period as approximately 9,849 hours, or a bit over 410 Earth days."

"That sounds awfully Earth-like," Kristen said. "It's shorter than Sawyer's World. If this planet *isn't* terraformed, that's a remarkable coincidence."

"I'm inclined to agree," said Rick, "especially since the rotation rate is a very Earth-like twenty-four hours, forty-six minutes."

"Shorter than a day on Sawyer's World," Kristen observed.

"Too close to be coincidence," Paul said. "That increases the likelihood that the lifeforms are Earth-descended. It's just as well George Darwin didn't come; he would have been disappointed. But for us, it means we're more likely to find useful biochemicals, which will make our sponsor happy."

"There are a few differences," Rick continued, "although nothing major."

"Such as?" Kristen asked. "Anything that will affect landing and take-off?"

"Mary and I have gone over that; she'll address it in a minute," Rick said. "The surface gravity is only ninety-nine percent of Earth's, but—"

"Not surprising, since the planet is smaller," Corey interrupted.

"Actually," Rick continued, "it *is* surprising, because the planet is denser than Earth, with an average density of about 5.6 compared to Earth's 5.5."

"So, a higher proportion of heavier elements," Kristen said, "probably meaning a larger core. That fits with the star having a higher metallicity than our own sun."

"That means the gravity falls off more rapidly with altitude," Mary said. "That's good."

"There's something else. The atmosphere is denser too, with a surface pressure twenty percent higher than Earth's at sea level. There's more oxygen in the atmosphere—"

"As we've already discussed," Corey said, interrupting again.

"—and nearly twice as much argon. Even at STP, standard temperature and pressure, the atmosphere would be more dense than Earth's air."

"Will that cause a problem?" Paul asked.

"It's breathable," Corey said. "If there's anything toxic that we can't detect from orbit, we'll find it when we get down and take samples. If so, it will be in low enough concentration that filter masks should take care of it." He turned to Mary. "Anything else?"

"To go back to Kristen's question," Mary said, "the atmospheric density will make entry and descent easier. There'll be more drag to slow us down. We'll have to descend at a shallower angle so as not to overtax the heat shield, but it won't be a problem. On the other hand, the higher drag is a drawback when we're climbing back to space. The lower gravity will help."

Paul nodded. That was what he had hoped. "Okay, *bien.* Figure out our latitude range—" the planet's rotation, fastest at the equator, would help with launch, that's why the Kourou launch site was where it was "—and then let's start looking for a landing spot."

"Aren't we going to deploy drones?"

"I'd like to save those to check out the landing area. We want to retain one as backup in case the first landing target is problematic." The drones only had a limited range.

"Can we spare one for a closer look at somewhere we won't land? We have three," Kristen said.

Paul considered this. Data had value. It might be worth it, but not at the expense of being able to land.

"How about this," he said. "If we get a good landing spot and still have a drone left, we can deploy that over the most interesting area that you determine. We'll stay in orbit until we get the data back from it."

"That works for me."

"Don't take too long," Mary said. "We don't want weather conditions at the landing area to change in the meantime. And the drones have limited battery life."

"Good points," Paul said. "All right, let's get to work."

∞ ∞ ∞

Aboard Jules Verne

Because of the cloud and drifting algae layers, building up a good map of the planet had been a laborious process of piecing together radar scans, images taken through gaps in the clouds, and some guesswork. At a rough estimate, the planet was two-thirds ocean covered, with the ocean more evenly distributed than Earth, and smaller continents. There were two large landmasses and three smaller ones—Kristen refused to acknowledge any of them as continents without more data about crustal plates and composition—as well as a scattering of "significant" islands ranging from New Zealand to Greenland sized.

The larger continent, or landmass, occupied nearly half the northern hemisphere, wrapping over the pole where it had accumulated a significant ice cap. Kristen imaginatively designated this "Landmass A." The other, "Landmass B," straddled the equator along a roughly northwest-southeast axis from 60 degrees north to 60 degrees south, with the southern portion also branching westward to curve toward the Landmass A. Since it was mostly split from the bulk of Landmass B by a sea, she designated it

"Landmass C," although allowed as how that could change depending on whether that sea was just a shallow flooded area like the Western Interior Seaway that had, during Earth's Cretaceous, covered the Great Plains of North America, or whether it was a deeper body, like the Mediterranean between Europe and Africa.

Paul's interest, however, had been captured by a network of lakes in the northern half of Landmass B, the largest of which, being roughly elliptical at 300 km by 75 km, and draining into a large river that flowed west and north to the ocean, bore a remarkable resemblance to a lake that he, Mary, and Rick were well familiar with.

"It looks like Lake Ontario," Rick had said.

"You're right," Paul agreed, "and that river could almost be the St. Lawrence. I didn't notice the similarity at first, since none of the other Great Lakes are there."

"That would have been too freaky."

"I wonder if the geology is similar," Kristen said. "Can we land there?"

Paul had his doubts because of the terrain, and the biologist, Corey, voiced another reason why not. "I'd rather land near an ocean," he said. "I want to get samples of both saltwater and freshwater life."

"Agreed. Let's find a spot near a seacoast, but with a river or freshwater lake nearby. What is it like near the mouth of that new St. Lawrence?"

"New St. Lawrence? Is that what we're calling it?" Rick said. "I suppose you're going to name the lake New Ontario?"

"*Merde*, no. Let's call it Lake Quebec," Paul said with a grin. "And the river is just New Lawrence, no Saint."

Rick shook his head. "Me and my big mouth. I hope those names don't stick."

Chapter 18: Orbital Survey

Orbiting Delta Pavonis III

Rick and Kristen were reprogramming the drones' flight computers for this planet's different gravity and atmosphere. The drones were vaguely insectile, like dragon flies, with broad thin wings that absorbed sunlight to extend the battery life.

"Do you think that green slime is going to cause a problem?" Rick said.

"You mean the aerophytoplankton?" Kristen said. Corey had determined that the green in the atmosphere was a layer of floating vegetation, and the only thing that made sense was some kind of algae held aloft by winds. They'd know for sure when the drones got down for a closer look.

"Yeah, that. These drones will have to descend through it to get a good look at the surface. If it builds up it will spoil their aerodynamics, and even if not, it will cut the available light."

"Do you have another suggestion?"

"Well, no."

Mary had been looking on, and spoke up. "Aerodynamically, a layer of green slime would be like ice buildup from flying through icing conditions, wouldn't it?"

Rick thought about it and nodded. "Probably not as bad. But it's not going to melt off by applying the heaters. It probably wouldn't be brittle enough to break off by flexing the de-icing boots, which these things don't have anyway."

"So, modify the programming to recognize the weight and drag gain from a surface buildup, but to ignore the temperature sensors. It should modify its flight model to account for 'ice' buildup without wasting power on de-icing."

Rick thought it over. "Yeah, okay, that should work. Just so long as it doesn't build up over the sensors. There's not much point in sending these down if they can't see."

"Or the green stuff could have no effect at all," Kristen said, "and you'll have worried for nothing. But maybe we keep one of the lens covers closed, or rig something over it, until we're below the weed layer or we completely lose vision in the other camera."

"You mean like an eye patch?" Rick said. "I like it. These things would look like sky pirates."

"Aye, matey," Mary said, with a very bad pirate accent.

Rick rolled his eyes and shook his head.

∞ ∞ ∞

The drone's orbital entry was nominal, and as it descended through the atmosphere, they caught glimpses of a tree-covered landscape through gaps in the clouds and floating green plankton.

There were scattered high clouds, and as the drone dropped below their level, the details of the green layer became clearer.

"It looks like a green dust," Corey said. "See the way it billows and swirls near those cumulous clouds?"

"The winds aren't very strong at this level," Mary said. "The drone's ground speed is close to its airspeed. What's keeping that dust aloft? Especially as it circulates through those clouds. Moisture would condense out on it and make it heavier."

"That's a great question. I wish we had a way to take a sample of it for a close-up look."

"We can do that after we land," Paul said. "The question is, will this stuff be a problem for us?"

"I think the only way to answer that is to fly the drone through it and see what happens. Or do we want to find and descend through a clear area first, then fly under it?"

"I'm having flashbacks of my early flying days," Mary said.

"Oh?"

"Doing something stupid, like flying above a cloud deck when you're not on IFR—Instrument Flight Rules."

"You mean, VFR on top, I think it's called?"

"Yeah. Illegal in Canada, and subject to restrictions in the US. It's fine if you know there will be holes in the clouds when you get where you're going. Less fine if there aren't and you have to fly through the cloud deck. Problem is, as a bush pilot, there might not be anyone where you're going to tell you what the ceiling is, and your aircraft is too old to have ground-visualizing radar. You start descending through the clouds, waiting to come out underneath, only to find out that the ceiling happens to be at local ground level, and you're trying to fly through a cumulo-granite cloud."

"Ouch," Rick said. "Obviously, that never happened to you."

"No. I had someone telling me the ceiling was at a thousand meters, so, plenty of room. But I began to get nervous when I had descended to nine-fifty with no signs of it clearing. I figured I'd give it another couple of hundred before climbing back through it and trying something else. It cleared up somewhere around eight hundred. This in an area where there were hills to several hundred meters."

"Let's not do that," Paul said. "But we did see some gaps in the clouds, so let's go through one of those, grab contingency data, and then try flying the drone through this weed or whatever it is and see what happens. The radar should keep us clear of any hills. If we lose the drone due to weed buildup, at least we'll have *some* data. If we don't, we'll know we can probably fly through it without serious problems. Agreed?"

Nobody had a better plan, so Mary commanded the drone to turn back toward where they had last seen a break in the clouds.

∞ ∞ ∞

Orbiting Delta Pavonis III

"So, we're agreed that Site Two is our best landing spot?" Paul asked the others. They had, but he wanted to give them all one last chance to voice an objection before committing to the landing.

"I would have preferred somewhere closer to the equator for orbital mechanics reasons," Mary said, "but we've been through that. I'm okay with Site Two."

"It's a compromise," Corey said, "but one we all agreed on. Let's get down there."

The others murmured agreement.

"Very well, let's make it so."

"Okay then," Mary said, pulling herself over to her pilot's seat and strapping in. "Stations, everyone."

Corey and Kristen made their way to their lower deck stations while Paul and Rick also strapped into the control chairs. Paul didn't really have a role in this except to oversee his pilot and navigator, and while he had cross-trained for both positions, they were far more experienced than he was. That was all right with him. As his father was fond of saying, "*Si vous ne savez pas ce que vous faites, engagez quelqu'un qui le sait; même si vous savez ce que vous faites, cela peut payer de déléguer.*" (If you don't know what you're doing, hire someone who does; even if you *do* know what you're doing, it can pay to delegate.)

The thrusters fired, gently nudging the *Jules Verne* to its new orbit, inclined enough to the equator to take it over the designating landing site twice per orbit, once tracking northeastward, then later, as the planet rotated beneath, tracking southeast.

With the orbit achieved, and confirmed by Rick's star sightings, Mary began maneuvers for entry.

Chapter 19: First Landing

Delta Pavonis III

Having done two previous landings, on Kakuloa and Taprobane, their entry into the new planet's atmosphere was almost routine. After an extended burn to kill the *Verne*'s orbital velocity and lower the altitude, the ship began to drag against the upper atmosphere, creating an orange glow as the energy of the *Verne*'s passing heated and ionized the air. As the ship dropped deeper into the atmosphere, the glow brightened and grew thicker, heating up as it absorbed the spacecraft's kinetic energy. They began to feel weight again as the drag increased, then the glow began to fade.

"First braking burn," Mary announced, as the ship's rocket engines fired to further slow its descent. By now, the orange glow had faded completely.

"The sky is blue, not green," Rick said, watching the view out the windows. He was looking toward the horizon; above them, it was still dark.

"For now. Wait until we hit the algae layer, in about four minutes."

The sound of the air rushing past the hull increased as they descended, punctuated by brief bursts of the attitude jets to correct the ship's path. "Trajectory nominal, going subsonic," Mary reported. "Still on the beacon."

"Altitude?"

"Coming through fourteen thousand meters now. Weed layer is at three thousand."

They continued falling for another minute, slowing to its terminal velocity. A few wisps of green flashed by the windows, and then they were into it. The windows grew darker, then there came a yellow flash, and the ship shuddered with a muffled *WHUMP!*

"*What was that?* Damage report," Paul yelled.

"No idea. Board is still green." The thrusters fired briefly to compensate for the jostling the ship took.

Then, "Landing gear deploying. Down and locked."

"Landing burn."

The engines roared with a burst of power, the ship slowed abruptly, and then settled to the surface with a thump, about the same force as whatever had happened while flying through the weed layer.

"Engines off. Attitude is stable." Mary said. "The *Jules Verne* has landed."

∞ ∞ ∞

"*Bien*. Run a full status check," Fabron ordered. "I want to know what that thump and flash was just before landing. Did we get hit by lightning?"

"Running that now," Mary said, "but it didn't feel like lightning. Been there, done that, and the electromagnetic pulse lights up the panel until everything resets. That didn't happen here, and there were no damage indications."

"It happened as we were going through the green layer," Rick said, "the aerophytoplankton. Maybe related?"

"That could be," Paul said. He switched to the intercom; his biologist was on the mid-deck. "Corey, could that flash and bang we experienced be related to the airborne algae?"

"That depends on what keeps them aloft," came the reply. "If it's more than the wind, like if they have gas cells that use methane or hydrogen as a lifting gas, then yes, our passing may have lit some of them off. Interesting biochemistry, if so; whatever enzymes they use to produce that could have commercial applications. I'll want samples."

That explanation sounded reasonable, and so long as there was no damage to the ship, it wasn't anything to worry about. "*Ç'est bien alors.* Okay, that means we can probably expect the same thing when we launch. Disturbing, but on the plus side, we may have just found our first licensable product."

∞ ∞ ∞

Jules Verne*, on Delta Pavonis III*

"I suppose you want the first footstep," Corey said to Paul. On the first Alpha Centauri missions, it had been the lead biologist who stepped out first, but by a similar tradition, naming rights also went to the first footer. It so happened that on Kakuloa and Sawyer's World, those first footers had been biologists, and the details of the landings on Spitzer and Taprobane had been, for different reasons, less than forthcoming.

"Of course," Paul said. "It's one reason I put this venture together. But we follow protocol first. Atmosphere tests, and then we go out in Biological Isolation Garments. Just as we planned."

In fact, Paul itched to set foot on the surface. He had no idea what he would say when he did, but it probably didn't matter. This would be at least the fifth extrasolar world humans had set foot on, so probably nobody would care what the first words were. He did, though, have an idea for the name. It had come to him as they approached the planet from space. He was not so impatient, however, as to ignore procedure. Even if the atmosphere were breathable, it wasn't necessarily healthy, and both Victoria Holmes and George Darwin had stressed the importance of initial isolation. He didn't want to bring anything potentially infectious aboard, nor did he—or more emphatically, Skrellan Pharmaceuticals—want to introduce to the planet any organisms that might destroy the local ecosystem, including any microorganisms the humans aboard might host.

Their first step would be to run a standard chemical analysis of the air. Their drone probes had already done this at a basic level, but the instruments aboard the *Verne* would go beyond the bulk composition and look not only at the gases, but also particulates, and look at those particulates for microbes and spores. Of course, the crew already knew the air contained live particulates; they had flown through a thick green layer of them during the descent.

They—mostly Corey—would also perform a suite of biological tests. The simplest of these was exposing a variety of culture dishes to the native atmosphere and seeing what, if any, organisms took hold. To help protect themselves, white mice, genetically modified to more closely resemble human physiology, would be similarly exposed, then closely monitored for ill effects. The whole procedure was more streamlined than what the *Chandrasekhar*'s team had gone through when they first landed at Alpha Centauri, but it would be twenty-four hours before anyone stepped out of the ship even in a Biological Isolation Garment—BIG—and those would stay on for at least a day after that, depending on the test results.

∞ ∞ ∞

Aboard Jules Verne, *next day*

"It is time, Paul said. "As we agreed, Corey and I will make the first, short, foray. Then Mary and Kristen, to set up the refueling apparatus. Sorry, Rick, you will have to wait your turn."

"That's okay," Rick said. "I can wait until we don't need the Barney suits anymore. Might be different if it were a real spacesuit, but those things just make me feel silly." He meant the required Biological Isolation Garments. The suits, lightly pressurized and brightly colored for visibility, were more magenta than purple, but somehow the nickname "Barney suit," inspired by a dinosaur from an old children's show, had stuck after one of the Centauri Expedition members had mentioned the resemblance.

"*Bien*. Speaking of Barney, Corey and I need to suit up."

∞ ∞ ∞

Paul and Corey finished donning their BIGs and checked each other's seals. They closed the inner airlock door and began the scrub procedure, flushing the airlock with a sterilizing gas and high-intensity ultraviolet light. They would do it again on their return. They wanted to avoid contamination, in either direction, until they'd had more time to check the effects of any earthly microbes they might have brought with them on samples of local life, and more importantly, any effects that local life might have on them. Paul glanced over at the white mouse, that had been exposed the day before, in its sealed cage within the airlock. It ran happily in its exercise wheel, so far showing no ill effects. *Tres bien*, Paul thought.

"Okay, scrub complete. We're go to open the outer door." Corey said.

"Opening." Paul checked that his safety lanyard was clipped to the handle beside the door and activated the lock. It swung open, and he stepped to the sill to take his first good look at the new planet. *His* planet, he couldn't help but think, although he knew that any such claim would be merely a footnote in the history books, and hopefully, royalty cheques from Skrellan Pharmaceuticals and the other companies Paon Co. had a contract with.

A hundred meters to the east, the meadow they'd landed on sloped down to a gravel beach. Paul could faintly hear the rumble of waves breaking on the shore, and he imagined he could smell the salt air. *Soon*, he thought. To the north, the meadow gave way to low scrub marking the edges of a river. He couldn't see it from his position in the airlock, but on the other side of the ship, he knew that the meadow was bounded by the jungle that seemed omnipresent on most of the land surface of this world. He glanced up at the overcast sky, the clouds streaked with skyweed green. They looked like they were drifting inland, and indeed he could make out a few patches of blue through the clouds farther out to sea. The sea itself was more green than blue, no doubt with its own algal growth, although not the bright green of pond scum. *Probably too much wave action for that*, he thought, but Corey could figure it out. With any luck, in all that vegetation, they'd find *something* of interest to the pharmaceutical companies.

"Are you going to stare at it all day?" came Corey's voice from behind, gently urging him to get a move on.

"All right. Patience, my friend. I'm going." Paul checked his safety reel again and, holding the bar by the hatch, swung himself out to step onto the ladder, then began climbing down. Above him, Corey stepped up to the sill and began staring out himself.

∞ ∞ ∞

Paul reached the foot of the ladder and paused again. The blast of their landing exhaust had charred and partly torn up the ground immediately below him, but the ship itself seemed intact, with only a little more wear to the heat shield than they'd seen after landing on Taprobane. The thin vegetation beyond the scorched circle could well have been grass, but that might only be convergent evolution. He'd leave the determination to Corey; *he* was the biologist.

He extended a leg to step off the ladder, wondering what his first words should be, or if it even mattered. Would anyone care what he said? He himself couldn't recall what any of the other first-footers, beyond George Darwin's "And so life from Earth takes its first step out into the galaxy," remembered more for its ultimate irony than its profundity.

Screw it, he decided. "I'm stepping off the ladder," he said, suiting action to words. As he put his foot down onto the surface of the planet, he added, "*En mémoire du capitaine Daniel, je touche la surface,*" (in memory of Captain Daniel, I touch the surface), making a very bad pun on the name of Captain Daniel de la Touche, the first Frenchman to seriously explore, back in 1604, what would become French Guiana.

∞ ∞ ∞

Paul returned to the ship after a half-hour of checking the ship and then wandering around the landing site watching Corey take preliminary samples. The vegetation, and the landscape, all had a vague "familiar yet different" feel. He entered the airlock, carrying Corey's biological samples with him. Mary and Kristen were already suited up in their BIGs, eager to get out on the surface themselves.

"I would suggest running the refueling hose to the river to the north," he said. "The water will be slightly fresher than directly from the sea."

"Except when the tide comes in," Kristen said.

"The filters can handle a bit of salt," Mary pointed out, "just like on Taprobane. Anyway, the seawater will have a higher fraction of deuterium."

"At these latitudes, the difference should be negligible," Kristen said, "but I can check that."

"Since we don't yet know the exact composition of the seawater here," said Paul, "let us be cautious until we know there's nothing that will poison the reverse osmosis membranes."

"I'll make that a priority," Kristen said. "Meanwhile, we can set the pumps to run only during ebb tide."

"*Bien.* I'll have Rick calculate a local tide table. Okay, off you go. Keep an eye on Corey, too. I don't want anyone wandering off by themselves, or straying out of sight of the ship, until we're sure the area is clear of dangerous animals."

"The noise of our landing will have scared anything off."

"Large animals with hearing, perhaps, but they'll be back. I want you to carry weapons when away from the ship. I hope we never have to use them, but if you wonder why, the report on the Chinese expedition to Epsilon Eridani is in the ship's library." It wasn't the official report, of course; China had never issued one. But *UDT* intelligence services had pieced together the story. The Chinese ground team had been savagely attacked by something like dire wolves, with one casualty. They had gotten off so lightly because the team had been armed. Paul, thanks to his—or his father's—contacts, had managed to acquire a copy of the report. [*[footnote? See "Alpha Centauri: The Return"]*]

He continued. "Your BIGs should be tough enough to protect against the local equivalent of insect bites or stings, perhaps even snakebites, but that's no reason not to be careful."

"Roger that," Mary said.

∞ ∞ ∞

The process of deploying the refueling hoses was much the same as it had been on Taprobane, although this time, no handy boulder camouflaged any existing hose couplings. Mary had often had to refuel planes herself at isolated airstrips back in Nunavut; attaching the hoses to the *Verne*'s fill ports wasn't drastically different.

Kristen made a few *pro forma* complaints about being the one to have to deploy the wet end, but she actually welcomed the opportunity to grab a few rocks from the beach and samples of the seawater. They would give her something to analyze in the first days when they were confined to or near the ship.

Chapter 20: Exploration and Findings

Jules Verne *landing site, Delta Pavonis III*

The team had been exploring without the cumbersome Biological Isolation Garments for a full day after Corey had given the "all clear" on the biological screening tests. The lightweight aircar components had been unloaded and partially assembled. Rick and Paul expected it to be ready to fly by late the next day.

"For all the good it will do us," Corey said. "Is there anywhere to land it within range?"

"It's not that bad," Kristen said. "We can make forays up and down the coast and land on the beach."

"There are also some clearings in the jungle," Mary added.

"Not of much interest to a geologist, though," Kristen said. "I'd like to visit some mountains or one of the desert areas we spotted from orbit."

"Out of range of the aircar," Paul said, "and too risky to try landing the *Verne* there."

"There'd be flat areas in a desert."

"But no water. We want to be sure we can refuel."

Kristen snorted. "That's one thing not lacking here. Ocean aside, with all the jungle inland, this place reminds me of what

Mary said about some of the early ideas about Venus. Wet, jungly, rainy, humid, and stinky."

"Or Dagobah," Rick said.

"You and your Star Wars references," Mary chided. "They bear no relation to reality."

"And wet Venus does? But what about the surprising number of Earth-like planets in Star Wars?"

"They weren't terraformed; they just happened."

"That was never stated in canon."

"All right, guys, that's enough," Paul said. "The rest of us don't want to hear this again."

"Besides," Mary said, "banthas and tauntauns are clearly not descended from Earth life."

"Oh, I don't know," Corey started, "they could—"

"I said *enough*. Look, I like science fiction as much as the next person, but we're sitting here on a real extrasolar planet orbiting a real star, with some real mysteries. Let's discuss those."

"Mysteries? Like what?"

"Like what is making that damned incessant hooting? Kristen said. "Corey says it isn't an owl."

"It's not," the biologist said. "I can't completely rule out that whatever it is descended from an ancient *Strigidae*—owl family—ancestor, not until I catch one. But, while I'm no ornithologist, it seems to me that the range of tones in those hoots is far more than any Earthy owl. Besides, we hear them both day and night; owls are mostly nocturnal."

"I've heard owl hoots in daylight," Mary said. "It's not that unusual."

"He's right, though," Kristen said. "It's more musical than owl hoots. Probably some either kind of bird, maybe more than one."

"I don't know," Rick said. "It sounds to me more like someone playing a flute . . . or maybe an ocarina."

That drew a round of laughter from the others.

"A very out-of-tune flute," Paul said.

"And that is why you make a better astronomer than a biologist," Mary said, "or a musician."

"He kind of has a point," Corey said, coming to Rick's defense. "It may not be birdsong at all. Other animals can make sounds like that. Too melodious for crickets, but maybe it's frogs."

"Frogs would fit with the swamp-world thing," Rick agreed, hastening to change the subject. "What about it, Paul? You haven't exercised your naming rights yet. *Are* you going to call this world Dagobah?"

Paul glared at him. "I most certainly am *not*." He paused, then grinned and said, "Actually, I was thinking of Verdigris."

"Verdigris, like the greenish salts on corroded copper?" Kristen asked.

"Exactly. Green decay. It fits, no?"

The others weren't sure if this was another of Paul's jokes or not, but none of them felt up to arguing the point.

∞ ∞ ∞

Two days later

"How about down there?" Corey suggested, pointing to a relatively clear area atop a ridge. He and Kristen were in the aircar, some eighty kilometers northwest of the landing site. Kristen wanted different terrain both for rock samples, and for placing a seismometer, and he sought a change in the flora and fauna for his own sampling.

"That looks good," she said as they drew closer. "Land on top, I can see a route down to that outcrop." The level ground at the top sloped gently away to the west, with a sharper drop on the east side. Below the crest, exposed rock showed clear sedimentary layering.

The craft wobbled as they crossed the ridgeline, caught in an updraft as the prevailing wind stumbled over the terrain. "Sorry about that," Corey said as he hit the autostabilizer switch.

"Just for that, you can help me dig the hole for the seismometer."

"Fine." He brought the aircar to rest a good ten meters from the edge and shut the motors down. "So, what first?"

Kristen had dismounted and was pulling her gear from the back seat, including coils of climbing rope. "I want you to belay me while I check that outcrop," she said, securing the end of one rope to the frame of the aircar. "And best to do that before you wear yourself out digging."

"Fair enough." He secured the other line and helped Kristen with her harness, then went to inspect the cliff edge while she grabbed her hammer and sample bag. The low vegetation, vaguely grass-like, grew up to the edge, revealing a thin layer of soil over a slightly crumbly layer of rock. Farther down, the rock was more solid. Satisfied that it wouldn't fray the tough climbing rope, he called back to Kristen. "Looks good. Whenever you're ready."

She finished tying herself in and stepped back to the edge. "On belay!"

"Belay on," Corey acknowledged, taking the strain as Kristen leaned backwards over the edge and stepped out and down.

He had payed about three meters of line when Kristen called, "Hold!"

He held, feeling the line squirm and tug as Kristen reoriented herself, then he heard hammering. Whether that was her placing a piton or chiseling a sample loose, he couldn't tell, nor did it matter. He wasn't holding her weight; the rope did that. He used friction to control its motion, or lack thereof.

The hammering stopped, and a few moments later came her call of "Continuing down, belay!"

The process repeated several times until finally, she yelled back, "Okay, that's it, coming back up! Climbing!"

She pulled herself up, climbing the rock or using the static rope while Corey took up the slack on the belay line. A few minutes later, she scrambled back over the edge. "Off belay," she said, panting slightly.

"Find anything interesting?"

"It's pretty much all sedimentary rock. I did see what looked like trilobite fossils but couldn't reach them. I'll belay you if you want to try."

"*What?* You—" then he caught her half-smile. "Oh, ha ha. Very funny." Trilobites had gone extinct on Earth some 250 million years ago, long, *long* before the Terraformers had collected the specimens they'd used to seed worlds with. Any such find would shake things up as much as the original discovery of terrestrial life beyond Earth had. No way would Kristen just leave such fossils behind.

"Okay, joker," Corey said. "I'm going to go collect some real specimens while you stow your climbing gear. Give me a holler when you figure out where you want the seismometer and I'll help you dig."

"Roger that."

∞ ∞ ∞

Kristen took a minute to catch her breath after the climb. Normally a twenty-meter climb wouldn't have bothered her at all, but none of them had been exercising as vigorously as they should have to stave off the effects of over a week in zero-gee, plus the several days before that. At least the gravity on this planet wasn't any higher than Earth's.

She gathered up the ropes and carried the gear back to the aircar. Corey was thirty meters off, periodically stooping down to examine something, or picking a plant and stowing it in a sample bag. Suddenly he froze, leaning over slowly, staring intently at, for all she could tell, nothing but yet another plant, just like the others. She went to look.

"What have you found?" she asked as she got closer. He half-turned and waved her to silence, not taking his eyes off of whatever he was peering at.

"A beetle," he stage-whispered. "A big one." He reached into his satchel with one hand and rummaged around for something, coming up with a sample vial about five centimeters in diameter and ten long.

Well, Kristen thought with some relief, *it can't be* that *big*. She eased closer, not wanting to startle Corey's prey, until she could see it. It was fairly large, mostly abdomen, like any beetle, with a mottled dark brown carapace. From what she could see of it, resting on a leaf, the head, thorax, and legs were more like that of a large ant, but with smaller mouthparts.

Corey had the vial open in front of the beetle, the opening toward it, as if hoping it would crawl in of its own accord. The beetle showed no interest in doing so, remaining motionless on the leave.

"Come on, in you go," Corey said in a low voice, bring his other hand to the insect's rear as if to nudge it forward.

"Should you be doing that? What if it—"

"Beetles don't have stingers. Hush," Corey said. He reached to prod it again. There was a *POP!* and *HSSS!* and Corey jumped back as if scalded, dropping the vial and waving his other hand.

"*OW! SHIT!* Damn that's hot!" He began blowing on his fingers.

The beetle had disappeared.

"Are you all right?" Kristen closed the distance between them. He had a yellowish fluid on his fingers, and as he reached his hand toward his mouth again, she grabbed it. "Don't!"

He pulled his hand away and started waving it again. "I wasn't going to put it in my mouth. I'm not *that* stupid. But it's hot." He stumbled toward the aircar.

She hurried ahead of him and grabbed a water bottle from the vehicle. "Hold out your hand," she said, pouring water over it when he did so.

"That wasn't a sting?" she asked.

"No," he muttered through gritted teeth. "Probably some kind of bombardier beetle." He wiggled his fingers under the stream of water. "Thanks, that helps."

"You didn't get any in your eyes?"

"No, fortunately not. It's a short-range defense, and my fingers got most of it. I was stupid."

"What defense?"

"Something like a bombardier beetle. Maybe exactly like. There are several hundred species on Earth. It's a defense against predators. They have internal reservoirs of hydroquinone and hydrogen peroxide in their abdomens. When threatened, they mix them together and, well, you saw. Pop, pop, fizz, fizz, oh what a relief it is. For the beetle, not the predator. Well, the beetle's butt probably gets warm too. That fluid comes out at near boiling."

"Are you going to be okay?"

"Yeah, it's mostly just a scald. The chemicals are rinsing off."

She held his hand up to examine the fingertips. The skin was discolored but didn't look perforated. "Okay, I guess you'll live."

"I'm fine," he insisted.

"Good. Otherwise, I might have thought you were trying to get out of digging the hole for my seismometer."

"Oh, for . . . Yeah, okay."

"I'm kidding, I've got it. You finish getting your hand cleaned off and put a covering on it. But I'm doing the flying on the way back."

"Thanks. I do want to see if I can get one of those beetles, though. I'd love to know the exact biochemistry, as I'm sure would our sponsors."

"Now *you're* kidding, right?"

"I'm not, but I don't mean today. I think I'll come back wearing a BIG."

∞ ∞ ∞

Verne *landing site*

"What have you got there today, Corey?" Mary Kalvak had found their biologist examining a small furry animal he had trapped earlier.

"I haven't come up with a name for it yet. It's some kind of rodent, though."

"Can it tell us anything interesting about this planet?"

"Funny you should ask. I'm about to set up the scanner so I can look at its skeleton. George Darwin once told me that he finally became convinced that something was weird with the biology on Kakuloa when he found that his 'runny babbit' had seven neck vertebrae."

Mary knew that Corey had been one of Darwin's students. In fact he was here on Darwin's recommendation, but the rest of it was lost on her. "And that's significant why?"

"Earth mammals all have seven neck, or cervical, vertebrae. Well, with one or two exceptions. Convergent evolution could explain fur and even general body plan, but that was too much of a coincidence. Why seven, and not six, or nine? After that, he started looking for evidence that would prove Kakuloan life was *not* descended from Earth life. Obviously, he didn't find any." Corey worked as he spoke, and he now had the scanner set up.

"Okay," he said, "here we go."

Within a few seconds, an image of the animal's skeleton began to appear on the scanner's screen. It would take a few minutes more to clarify and the details of soft tissues began to resolve, but it sufficed for Corey's purpose.

"Let's see. One, two, . . . five, six. Six? That's odd."

Mary wasn't convinced; the image was still blurry. She looked closer, watching as the image came into better focus. "No, look, that one is actually two. They're just thinner. See?"

Corey double-checked. "Okay, you're right. Seven. Order *Mammalia*. No surprises there." He scanned the rest of the skeletal image for confirmation. "The teeth are a bit weird, though."

"So, it's got big teeth. You said it was some kind of rodent."

"I'm not talking about the front teeth. Look here." He zoomed in the image, centering it on the animal's jaw. The rear tooth on each side was quite large, the equivalent of several teeth in the jaws of most animals Mary was familiar with.

"Those *are* big teeth," she said. "Like the, what, molars? are fused together. No, sharper than molars. A mutation?"

"I don't think so," Corey said, thoughtful. "At least, not recently. Try a hundred million years ago."

"What?"

"I'll need to check, both with other specimens and my references, and I could be wrong on the age. It might be older than that. But I think we're looking at a multituberculate. The paleontologists are going to love this!" He was already checking the ship's database on his omni as he finished talking.

"A multi what? I thought you said it was a mammal, not a dinosaur."

"No, no, not a dinosaur. There were mammals around even during the Jurassic, but not many of them, and small. A multituberculate is, or was, a kind of mammal. Here we go." He began reading from his omni screen. "'Multituberculata is an extinct taxon of small rodent-like mammals—' blah, blah '—first appeared in the Jurassic period . . . survived the K-T extinction . . . died out 45 to 50 million years ago.' Fascinating. So, they overlap the time frame when the Terraformers were transplanting life from Earth. I wonder why we haven't found multituberculates on any of the other planets." So far, all life found on terraformed planets could be traced to progenitor species from shortly after the extinction event that had wiped out the non-avian dinosaurs —and many other species—on Earth. How they had been transplanted, and who had terraformed the planets in the first place, remained a mystery.

"Possibly for the same reason there are no grasses on Kakuloa," Mary said. It was one of the biological factoids she remembered. "Whatever reason that is."

Chapter 21: Surprises

Jules Verne *landing site*

The next day the team awoke to a steady downpour of rain. They sat under one of the tent canopies they'd set up at the landing site, drinking coffee. Despite the weather, they all preferred it to the confines of the ship in which they'd spent so much time.

"I told you this place was like a wet Venus," Mary said, staring out at the rain dripping off the canopy. "The good news is that I think it will taper off by tonight."

"You think?" Rick asked. "Aren't pilots supposed to understand weather?"

"Give me a proper weather map, sure. The satellite images of clouds obscured by skyweed are only marginally helpful without barometric readings and wind directions."

"What about the weather stations Kristen placed at her seismometer sites?"

"They are all to the west. This front came in from the east, over the ocean."

"Well," Corey said, "I've got things to do here. Specimens to catalog. But when this lets up, I'd like to get out and see what critters the rain has brought out."

"It's not the desert," Rick said. "Do you think there'll be much difference between humid jungle and even more humid jungle, as far as the local wildlife is concerned?"

Corey shrugged. "You never know. And there'll be pools of water in leaves and flowers that can be breeding areas."

"So, more mosquitoes then?"

"Aren't you cheerful today?" Mary chided Rick.

"Sorry, I guess it's the rain."

"And yet you lived in Kingston for three years." The town often saw rain, thanks in part to the adjacent Great Lake.

"Well," Kristen said, "when this does clear up, I'd like to take the aircar down the coast a way, to check out the shoreline in that direction. Rick, do you want to join me?"

That perked him up. "Sure," he said. He looked around the table. "Does that fit with everyone's plans?"

Paul Fabron, who had been observing the exchange while quietly sipping his coffee, spoke up. "That's fine, if Mary goes with Corey. I'll stay here at the ship and try to stay out of trouble."

Mary shrugged without much enthusiasm, but said, "Yes, I suppose that works."

∞ ∞ ∞

Jungle, three km from landing site

Mary cursed as she swatted at yet another mosquito. "Dang it, the bugs here are even worse than back in Nunavut. Corey, do you have anything back in that lab of yours that would work as repellant?"

"I'll have to check, but there's always the old *coureurs des bois* recipe," Corey said. "A mixture of bear grease and skunk urine, as I recall. Not that I've seen either bears or skunks here yet."

"Ugh, no thanks. I'd rather suffer a few bug bites. You're sure there's no chance of malaria or yellow fever?"

"Not on this planet. None of the samples I took showed any signs of parasites or viruses that would infect humans. So far, there's nothing close to primates on this planet, so local diseases haven't evolved to our biology."

"That's something, anyway."

They hiked on a little farther, keeping to where the vegetation was thinner, with Mary in the lead.

"Hold up," Corey called, "I want to get some samples from down here."

Mary turned and looked back. Corey had fallen back about ten meters, and had bent down to reach some low-growing plants beneath the ubiquitous tall, thin bushes that grew between the trees. Mary didn't understand how anything could grow as thick as it did under the overhead canopy, especially with the light already dimmed by filtering through the skyweed. Corey had said something about adaptation and chlorophyll types responding to different wavelengths, but she hadn't really absorbed his explanation. This place differed from the northern forests she was used to, although there were resemblances to what they called "moose pasture" back home. So far, though, there hadn't been any signs of moose.

She turned her gaze toward the trail ahead. She hoped that somewhere out there they would find something to excite Skrellan Pharmaceuticals, for Paul's sake. Not that she would object to her share of whatever rewards Paon Co. might earn, but at least she was on salary, and this trip would make a nice addition to her logbook. She had considered becoming a star pilot, but was coming to the conclusion that the long stretches of boredom between stars might not be worth it. At least with flying aircraft, those stretches were never more than a few hours, not days. And then there was the boredom of wandering around an uninhabited planet. For her, the excitement had worn off quickly. The water from the previous day's rain, dripping from the leaves overhead, didn't help. Then she heard Corey yell, along with a loud rasping snarl.

∞ ∞ ∞

Mary whirled to see Corey on the ground, lying on his side, fighting off—*was that a bear?* The furred animal was as large as a small bear, perhaps a cougar, but fatter. She ran back toward him, unslinging her rifle while shouting at it, hoping to scare it off. It had pronounced teeth, not fangs like a sabertooth, but more like a beaver, only bigger and thicker. Corey had it by the neck, keeping the gnashing jaws away but being raked by the animal's claws. The two of them rolled, the animal pinning him beneath it.

She quickly dropped to one knee, aimed, and fired. The animal turned at the sound and flash of the shot, then reeled back, coughing blood, trying to flee. She fired again, finishing it, then rushed to attend to Corey.

"Where are you hurt? Did it bite you?" she said, checking him over for serious bleeding.

He pushed her away weakly. "I'm all right," he said. "Just a few scratches."

"Bullshit." She could see deep gouges in his right shoulder, and the bloody rips in his shirt suggested there were more on his back. She pulled a field dressing from the first aid kit in her pack and pressed it against the deepest scratches. Blood soaked it quickly.

"Ow, shit. That stings. Here, help me sit up."

"Not yet. I'm calling for help." They were close enough to the ship that she could signal Paul directly on his omniphone.

"*Oui?*"

"Paul, Corey's been injured. Animal attack. I killed the . . . whatever it was, but I may need help getting him back to the ship."

"*Merde.* Stabilize him while I call the others. Are you in a safe position?"

"I think so, just a moment." She looked at Corey. "What do you think, will there be more of those around?"

He darted a look at her, eyes wide, then at the surrounding bush, then back at the animal. "Pack predators are usually in more open terrain than this, so they can coordinate. Hard to do that in a forest. We're probably fine." He said the last through gritted teeth as he winced in pain.

"We're okay for now," she reported back to Fabron. "But hurry."

∞ ∞ ∞

The beach, south of the landing site

Rick strolled along the beach above the tide line. Nearby, Kristen knelt at a rock outcrop, prying loose a sample with her geologist's hammer. He kicked idly at the stones as he walked, stopping occasionally to watch Kristen, or to pick up interesting-looking rocks, then toss them into the sea. One very different from the others caught his eye.

It looked like a fragment of pottery, smaller than his fist but thin, with a curve. He didn't think much of it at first; beaches on Earth were often littered with shards of old ceramics, or pieces of sea glass or driftglass. He was about to toss it away when an alarm shrilled from the aircar, signaling a radio message.

He headed back toward the vehicle, but Kristen was closer, and she was already on the call when he got there.

"Right," she said into the microphone, "we'll be there ASAP. Less than ten minutes."

They were twenty-five kilometers from the *Verne*. To cover that in ten minutes would take the aircar's top speed. Rick climbed in. He could ask questions on the way. Kristen was already in and spinning up the rotors.

"What's happening?"

"Corey's injured. Animal attack. Mary needs help getting him back to camp."

"Can we land there? Wherever *there* is?"

"About three klicks from the *Verne*, in the jungle. Probably not but we can look. Otherwise, we land by the *Verne*. Paul will be waiting with the stretcher."

"Sounds bad."

"We don't know that. Mary would be playing it safe. We'll find out in a few minutes."

As the aircar reached altitude, Kristen tilted it forward and pushed the throttle to maximum.

∞ ∞ ∞

In the jungle

"Help me sit up," Corey said.

"Are you sure?"

"Yes, besides, being upright will help stop the bleeding."

Mary wasn't sure about that, but as gently as she could, she helped him sit up. Sure enough, there were more gouges down his back, but not so deep. "Let me spray those," she said, reaching back into the first aid kit for the combination antibiotic and local anesthetic spray.

"Turn," she said. As she treated the wounds on his back, Corey peered at the remains of his attacker.

"Nice shot," he said. "Weren't you worried about hitting me?"

"Not from a kneeling position," she said. "It was above you. Something I learned about defense against polar bears."

"Really? Ever have to shoot a polar bear?"

"No, thank goodness. It was theoretical." She didn't like the look of his injuries. His back wasn't too bad, but blood had already soaked through the bandage on his shoulder. She kept talking to distract him. "What is that thing anyway? It looks like a giant beaver, although I never heard of beavers attacking other animals."

"Close, I think. Not a beaver, though."

"Some other rodent, then," Mary said, "of unusual size."

Corey gave her a quick smile. "Actually, from the close-up I got of its teeth, it's another multituberculate. Maybe something like a *Taeniolabis*, if I remember the species right. They were big, but not this big. It's going to be a pain to drag it back to camp; it must be well over a hundred kilograms."

"We've got to drag *you* back to camp first. The others are on their way. You're sure there aren't any more nearby?"

"I hope not. Probably not. A predator that big requires a lot of territory. But, I think I can walk."

"You sure it was a predator? Not a mama protecting her kits?"

"That one is male."

She looked at it again. It lay on its side, belly toward them. Yes, a male. "A protective papa, perhaps?"

"If so, then mama might be nearby. Let's get out of here. Help me stand up."

Mary considered arguing, but figured that would be futile. She put his left arm over her shoulders and heaved. With his cooperation, she got him to his feet, still supporting much of his weight. She looked at his face. He was pale, ashen.

"Maybe put me back down. Dizzy."

She lowered him to the ground, making him lie back instead of sitting. He didn't argue.

Her omni beeped. Paul.

"We're on our way," he said. "Be there in a few minutes. How is he?"

"Resting. He's suffering shock and blood loss, but he's mostly coherent. It can't be too bad." At least, she hoped not.

"*Bien*. See you shortly."

"Mostly coherent?" Corey muttered. "I think that's the nicest thing anyone's ever said about me."

"Hush. Now you're getting delirious."

Mary went through her first aid kit wondering if there were anything else she could do for him. Ironically, Corey himself had the most experience in that area. If they were days from help, she'd probably try to suture his shoulder wound, but that could wait until they got back to the ship's medical bay.

She packed up the kit and picked up her rifle again, holding it ready just in case Mama *was* around. She heard a rustling in the jungle nearby. She raised the rifle. "Who's there?" she called out.

∞ ∞ ∞

"It's us!" Paul called back. "Where are you?"

"Over here, keep following the trail."

Paul, Rick, and Kristen jogged a little farther down the trail, rounded a curve, and found them. Corey lay near the body of a bear-sized animal, a bloody bandage on his right shoulder and his shirt torn. Mary stood guard nearby, lowering her rifle as they came into sight.

Kristen knelt down, feeling Corey's forehead, and then checking his pulse. "Not bad. Let's get him on the stretcher."

Rick had been carrying the lightweight stretcher, rolled up, over his shoulder. He unslung it and, with Paul's help, set it up on the ground beside Corey. "Man," he said, "the lengths to which some people will go to avoid hiking back to camp."

"Heh," Corey started, then, "ow, don't make me laugh. I've got scratches along my ribs."

"At least you've still got your sense of humor," Rick said, maneuvering to take Corey's head and shoulders. "Paul you take his legs. Kristen, can you help with his waist? We need to get him onto the stretcher, and I don't want to put too much force on his right shoulder." As it was, Rick already had blood smeared onto his bush shirt. It couldn't be helped.

"Okay, on three," he said. "One, two, three." They managed to lift and drag Corey onto the stretcher. "Oof, you're a heavy dude."

"Can you guys carry him all the way back to camp?" Kristen wondered. "What if we each take a corner?"

"No," Paul said, "not all four of us, not with possibly more of those animals around. Mary stays on guard."

"You take that end," Rick said to Paul, gesturing at Corey's feet. "Kristen and I can split this end. We'll rest and rotate as needed. It's not that far."

"*Bien*, that works."

"What about the *Taeniolabis* carcass?" Corey said weakly. "Came all this way for specimens, pity to leave it."

Paul sighed. "I'll take a few photographs and some samples. We can come back later and see what the scavengers have left." He pulled out his omni and began taking pictures of the beast.

Corey turned slightly to watch, wincing at the motion of his injured flesh. "Hopefully, bones at least," he said. "And the state will tell us more about what other creatures are around."

While Mary scanned the surrounds, listening and watching for any movement in the bush, weapon at the ready, Paul finished up as Corey directed.

Rick had to hand it to Corey; he certainly was dedicated.

Chapter 22: Newcomers

Verdigris, next morning

The shrill of his omni roused Paul Fabron from sleep. A dim light showed through the cabin window, and the time suggested that it was near local dawn. He silenced the alarm and looked at the screen. The ship was signaling about something, but he was *in* the ship. He got up and stumbled groggily to the control panel.

It showed an incoming alert message from one of the sub-satellites they'd left in orbit. He scanned it. It consisted of a brief dump of data it had logged, data that had been odd enough to trigger the "needs human attention" algorithm. He read it over twice, trying to grasp its meaning. Then he did. "*Merde!*" he muttered, then activated the ship's alarm system.

The raucous shriek had everyone roused in moments. "This is Paul. Come up to the bridge," he ordered over the PA.

"What's going on?" several of them asked as they stumbled in.

"*Regardez,*" Paul said as he put the alert message up on the main screen. He guessed that most of them wouldn't get it, but Mary would, and Rick might.

"What?" Corey said. His injuries, stitched up and with a covering of artificial skin, were beginning to heal nicely.

"It looks like another ship has arrived in-system," Mary said. Our sensors picked up thruster flares and electromagnetic disturbances."

"What ship?"

"We don't know that yet," Paul said. "We haven't received any messages from them. They may not even know we're here. We haven't kept it secret but neither have we advertised it."

"Are they in orbit? Can we spot them on telescope?"

"Probably not yet, and through the skyweed?" Rick said. "Are you joking?"

"They'll know we're here soon enough," Mary said. "We've got subsats that are broadcasting."

"Good point," Paul said. "The subsats will let them know we're here."

"Do you want to turn them off?"

"No. We still need their observation data, and I think we can use one to look for our new arrival. Is that right, Rick?"

"Maybe. We do have one sat with a telescope, but finding another ship with would be iffy. If it fires thrusters again, probably. If it enters orbit, it will depend on the parameters. The planet might be in the way."

"Why don't we just hail them and say hello?" Corey wondered.

"I think we'll let them make the first move," Paul said. "In the unlikely event they're hostile, it's probably better to keep our heads down."

"Hostile? Do you think that's likely?"

"No, I said not. But we don't know who they are. It could be that China has taken up interstellar exploration again. There's even a remote chance they're aliens. But it's more likely to be a *UDT* ship, either a private one or an official exploration ship."

"The *UDT* already knows we're coming here. Why send an exploration ship?"

Paul shrugged. "Perhaps to check on us. Maybe they've changed the rules. Who knows? Or it could be my father telling me to come home. More likely, it's another private exploration effort. We don't know. And until we do, I think we're better off letting them make the first move. They will probably be hailing us as soon as they detect our satellites."

"What do we do until then, just wait?"

"Mostly. Rick and Mary, can you configure our subsats to look for that ship and monitor for additional drive or radio emissions? Nothing too blatant; don't go sending radar beams into deep space."

Mary nodded. "We'll see what we can do."

"*Merci.* Anyway, it's a big planet. Plenty for others to explore," Paul said, more cheerfully than he felt. To the team he added, "let's get some coffee going. I'm sure Rick and Mary will need it."

"Got that right," Mary muttered as she brought up the satellite interface on a control screen.

∞ ∞ ∞

Aboard the Matthew*, approaching Delta Pavonis III*

"It certainly is green," Sebastian Thorne said. "Have you decided on a name yet?"

It had already been decided that Captain Talbot would be planting the first footstep and get naming rights.

"Given the color," Talbot said, "I'm thinking 'New Ireland.' I'm part Irish on my mother's side. But let's not get ahead of ourselves. Have we seen any signs of intelligent life?"

"It's hard to get signs of anything through all that green crud," Thorne replied. "But no, there are no obvious traces of industrial contaminants in the atmosphere, and no radio emissions other than what you'd expect from lightning storms."

"Hold it," a crewman, monitoring for radio signals, said. "That's not the case. I'm picking up some kind of transmission."

"From the planet?"

"No, something in orbit. The signal is weak, probably beamed at the surface. It might be telemetry."

"Is it on a standard frequency?"

"Affirmative. A standard telemetry band."

"Then it's almost certainly human," Thorne said. "Somebody got here first, and they left survey satellites in orbit, just like we're planning to."

"Yes," the captain said. "There were rumors of another expedition headed out this way." Talbot knew they were more than rumors, but he didn't want to let on just how much he knew about Fabron and the *Jules Verne*. If it *was* them, they had made much better time than he had expected. He'd have to keep that in mind.

"Shall I hail them?" the radioman asked.

"Negative. Let's keep it quiet for now. Wait for them to hail us, and let me know if they do. Do not acknowledge without my say so. If they know we're here, they may bolt."

"Uh, roger that," the radioman said. There was puzzlement in his voice, but he knew how to follow orders. "Maintaining a listening out."

"How do you want to handle this, Cap'n?"

"Just as though there were nobody here. We survey the planet from orbit and pick out a landing spot. Let's pick one far away from whoever is down there, if anyone is. No point in exploring the same places twice."

"All right," Thorne said. "You heard the man. Let's set up for orbit."

∞ ∞ ∞

Jules Verne, *later that day*

"Anything to report?" Paul asked Rick. He and Mary had been taking turns monitoring the data coming in from their satellites, looking for further evidence of another ship in the system.

"Nothing since it looked like something entered orbit a few hours ago," Rick said. They had detected thruster burns then. "It's been quiet ever since. If they're still in orbit, they're not maneuvering or transmitting anything."

"So, no sign of atmospheric entry?" That would leave a plasma trail in the upper atmosphere.

"No, but they could have done that on the other side of the planet, or at least out of view of any of our sats. We don't have anything like complete coverage."

"*Eh bien.* It is curious that they didn't try hailing us. Surely they would have detected telemetry from our sats."

Rick shrugged. "I guess they don't want to talk."

That seemed obvious. The question troubling Paul was, *why not?* Perhaps for the same reason he hadn't wanted to hail them. Perhaps they'd be best to keep their heads down, collect their data, and get back quickly to file their claims. He doubted the other ship would come all the way here only to leave without touching down. Kristen was already conducting planetary scans with a mix of radar and lidar to penetrate the vegetation. He'd have her keep an eye out for their landing site.

Chapter 23: Unidentified Landed Object

Jules Verne, *control room*

Kristen Payne did a double-take as she examined the newest downloads from their mapping sub-satellite. She called up the images they'd taken of the area when they first arrived, then flipped back to the new ones. There was no mistake. "Captain," she called out, "you need to see this."

Paul stepped over to the console where she sat, and glanced at the screen over her shoulder. A clearing filled most of the frame, with the ever-present Verdigris jungle off to one side, and on the other, a body of water—there wasn't enough in the frame to tell if it was a lake or broad river, but it lacked the surf he'd expect of a seacoast. Near the middle of the clearing sat a triangular structure, longer than it was wide. Scattered around it were smaller objects, impossible to make out clearly at this resolution. He had a feeling he knew what it was, and he didn't like it.

His suspicions were confirmed when Kristen said, "It wasn't there when we arrived. I checked."

"That's a V-class starship, isn't it? Do you have a better resolution image?"

"No, but I can task one of the sats to take one on the next pass."

"Do it. Meanwhile. . . ." He went over to the main controls and picked up a microphone. Keying it, he said, "All hands, secure what you're doing and report to the control room. We have an issue."

"What are you going to do?" Kristen asked, turning from where she'd finished sending a command to her observation sats.

"I'm not sure yet," Paul said, "possibly nothing. How long until we get better pictures?"

"Three hours. We got lucky on the orbital track."

"If it is a ship, can you determine when it landed? Or entered the system?"

"I can review other images. We don't know how long it might have been in orbit before landing, or if it landed somewhere else first."

"Before *what* landed?" Rick McDonald had caught the tail end of the discussion as he arrived. "What's going on? Did we find the other ship?"

"I'll explain when the others get here," Paul said. "I don't want to repeat myself."

Rick cast a quizzical look toward Kristen, who leaned back from her console and pointed at the screen. He peered at it, then his eyes went wide. "Holy shi—"

Just then, Mary and Corey also arrived in the control room.

"Problems, boss?" Mary asked.

Paul started a nod, then changed it to a shrug. "Kristen," he said, "put that up on the big screen."

As she did so, he continued. "This just showed up on the mapping cameras. It wasn't there when we arrived. We should have a better image in a few hours. But does anyone *not* think this is a V-class starship, one that landed long enough ago for someone to start setting up camp around it?"

He looked at the faces examining the fuzzy image on the big forward screen, hoping to see a sign that *someone* had a better explanation.

"That's what it looks like to me," Mary said.

"Likewise," from Corey.

"Uh, maybe an *alien* spaceship? Like a very small Imperial Star Cruiser?" Rick said, his tone not serious.

"That's not helpful, Rick," Paul said, but the wisecrack had lightened the mood.

"What's the big deal?" Corey wondered. "We got here first. We should signal them and say hello."

"It's not a matter of who got here first," Paul said. "If they get back to Earth before we do, they'll claim it. And that ship is faster and perhaps with more range than this one."

"But we have pictures proving they weren't here when we arrived. Our claim should have precedence."

"They could say they landed somewhere else first, then it comes down to examining their logs and our logs," Paul said. "But as the law stands, it's a matter of who gets back to Earth and files a claim first."

"That's not fair!"

Paul shook his head. "Unfortunately, the law and 'fair' seldom coincide." He looked at Mary. "Is there any way to tell when they arrived in the system?"

"Not if they did arrive before us. But the sensors on our satellite array did pick something up. Unless there are *two* ships down there, it must have been that one."

"*Bon.* Go through our data and file copies of anything relevant. Rick, help her with that."

"Roger that."

"Corey, Kristen, how soon can you be ready to leave?"

"*What?* I've still got tons of studies to do," Corey said. "I thought we were staying for six weeks?"

"There's that desert to the northwest I'd like to check out," Kristen said. "It'd be nice to see some rock that wasn't covered in dirt and decaying vegetation."

"We're not leaving yet, but I would like the option of getting back to Earth first," Paul said. "Your studies might be academically interesting, but they won't be useful to our customers if we don't have a claim. If that means we have to leave tomorrow, then so be it."

"And if that other ship did get here first? You'd jump their claim?"

Paul didn't answer immediately. His sense of fairness said no, but if whoever the others were could afford a V-class ship, they weren't hurting for funds. His people, on the other hand, were counting on him to deliver. "As I said, the law and fair seldom coincide. If it were only me, then no, I probably would not. But I owe money for this expedition, including to all of you." He paused, surveying the faces of his crew. They looked as conflicted as he felt. He forced a smile and added, "But I think the data will show that we were the first to arrive."

The data did indeed seem to confirm that. The later, higher resolution images of the other ship's landing area showed they were still setting up a base camp. That encouraged Paul. If they'd been here less time than the *Jules Verne*, they would probably leave later. Maybe. He gave his science team a tentative two more weeks. "But try to keep most of your gear and samples in the ship, in case we have to pack up in a hurry," he added.

Chapter 24: Discoveries

Aboard Jules Verne, *some days later*
"Paul, come and look at this," Kristen said. She sat at one of the ship's secondary consoles, with imagery from one of their orbital passes showing on the screen.

"*Qu'est-ce que c'est?* What is it?" Paul said, coming to look over her shoulder.

"I was checking on the other ship when I first found these. The image is from the leaf-penetrating radar scan," she said. "It's not ideal, but between the jungle and the skyweed, it's the best image of the actual surface that we have. It also helps me find interesting geological features."

"I take it you found some? Tell me you didn't find another ship."

"No, the only other ship is on the far side of the planet, like they're avoiding us. As for interesting features, well, possibly. I first noticed something like this near that ship, but I've found more, closer. Take a look." She zoomed in until it showed what might be a cluster of rounded hillocks. "These," she said.

"What am I looking at?"

"Well, if this were glacial terrain, they might be drumlins, although they're too round. Drumlins are typically elongated in the direction of glacial flow. If it were tundra, they might be pingoes, hills formed by ice accumulation. But these are neither; they're too far from the poles."

"Cinder cones?" Paul said, guessing. He couldn't think of anything else that would make rounded hills like this. "How big are they?"

"No, the geology is wrong. This isn't anywhere volcanic. The whole area is overgrown. Also, they're more rounded than conical, at least as far as I can tell from the radar scan."

"Eroded, perhaps? Cinder cones would wear down quickly under rain and vegetation, wouldn't they?"

"They would, but these are the wrong shape. Too rounded."

"*Eh bien*, what are they?"

"I'm wondering if they're artificial," she said.

"You mean some kind of imaging artifact? Is there a problem with the radar?" Paul said. A radar problem that contaminated their data would greatly reduce its value, but that might be preferable to the alternative.

"No, I mean artificial as in somebody built them. They almost look like stone igloos, except larger. I'll need a close-up look to be sure."

"How far away from here are they?"

"I've found several clusters of these scattered around the planet, but the closest are one hundred thirty kilometers from here."

"You say somebody built these. Who? We didn't see any signs of civilization from orbit."

"I didn't say that. I said they *look* artificial. Even that doesn't necessarily imply built by intelligent beings—they could be the equivalent of beehives or beaver lodges—"

"Big beavers," Paul interjected.

"You saw the thing that attacked Corey. *Anyway*," she continued, "we barely saw *anything* from orbit, with all that skyweed. That's why I'm going over the radar scans. But you're right. There's no cleared land around these, and a city—if that's what these represent—needs agriculture to support the population. If these *are* buildings, the builders may be long gone."

Paul hoped so. The prospect of encountering another intelligent species, while exciting, could also mean that Verdigris might, like Taprobane, be declared off-limits. The fame that went with discovery was all very well, but his crew needed the money from licensing biopharmaceutical rights. If there was already a civilization here, that could be off the table.

"All right," he said. "Can you set up an automated image search for more of these? And for anything that looks like agriculture—plowed fields, terraces, orchards, that sort of thing. Also, other structures—corrals for animals, fishing weirs, anything like that. Let's see if there's anyone home."

Kristen looked doubtful. "That's pretty fuzzy search criteria. We'll probably get a lot of false positives. Shouldn't we check out what we've got first? Maybe these domes or hills are a natural phenomenon."

"We can do both. Set up a preliminary search to run in the background, then start planning an expedition to get a ground truth on whatever those things are. I'm not sure a drone would do it justice. You should probably go in person. But take somebody with you. No solo outings. And clear it with me first."

"Okay, copy that." She turned back to the console to begin programming the image search.

∞ ∞ ∞

Aboard Jules Verne, geology lab

Mary took one look at the aerial pictures of Kristen's drumlins, and said, "*igluvijaq*."

"What, now?"

"Well, they're obviously not, not in a jungle, but if those were on a snowfield, they'd be *iqluvijaq*, what you'd probably call igloos, although *iglu* itself just means house. *Igluvijaq* is the term for 'snow-house,' at least where I grew up in Nunavut."

"You're saying these are houses? Snow houses?"

"No, not snow, not in the jungle, of course. But the dome shape fits. And look at this one here—" she pointed to one picture that showed more detail and traced out a faint spiral line "—this suggests that it was built in the same way, laying out stone blocks in a spiral structure to form the dome. Run it through an edge enhancement filter."

"Not a natural phenomenon, then." Paul said, his tone serious. If there were intelligent natives on this planet. . . .

"Well, not geological, anyway," Mary said. "I'd argue that beaver lodges are natural phenomena, as are termite mounds. Neither would disqualify a planet for commercial use."

"They're awfully big and regular for anything like a beaver lodge or termite mound," Kristen objected. "But if they are stone, they could be thousands of years old. I've scanned for other signs of habitation—cultivated fields, fences, roads, and so on; anything that could build stone igloos could build those too —and found none. Also, everywhere I've found these things, they were overgrown. No signs of any new ones. If they *were* deliberately built, who or whatever built them isn't doing it anymore."

"Sawyer's World once had intelligent natives," Corey noted. "They found stone tools, spearpoints, and the like. They went extinct thousands of years ago. Maybe that happened here, too."

Paul nodded. "Not to wish ill on any intelligent species, but that would simplify our situation. Due diligence requires that we'll have to check out these drumlins, or igloos, or whatever they are. Perhaps there is a natural explanation, even a geological one. They could be artificial, but ancient. Or maybe they're molehills for some kind of giant alien moles."

"And I thought the rodents of unusual size were bad," muttered Corey.

"Let's make it a three-person expedition," Paul said. "But if there's any sign that there are still intelligent natives around, get out of there fast. We're not equipped or trained for first contact."

∞ ∞ ∞

They decided that the team would comprise Kristen, the geologist who discovered the domes, Corey, their biologist, both to take samples along the way and to help determine if the domes were built by some kind of animal or social insect. Paul Fabron exerted his authority and took the third position; if there was any sign that the domes were anything but natural, he wanted to be on the spot to make decisions. Artifacts from an extinct culture could be more valuable than any potential biopharmaceutical, but if the culture was *not* extinct, well, the *Union de Terre* regulations were unclear, but if Taprobane was an example, then *hands off!* would be the default option. Paul would hate to have Paon Company's assets seized because of some bureaucratic overreaction.

The nearest such domes were 130 kilometers away, with another group not quite 200. Too far and too dangerous to hike, but they had the aircar. Assuming there was somewhere to land it.

∞ ∞ ∞

Verdigris

It turned out there were several clusters of the strange domes within range of their aircar, although the closest such, some 130 km away, was so surrounded by dense vegetation that they couldn't see anywhere to land. Corey was all for not letting that stop him, apparently not having learned caution from the ROUS attack.

"What I'm saying is that the next closest cluster is nearly two hundred kilometers, that's a hundred and forty klicks farther round trip. That's an hour in the air. Why not just hover above the trees for that hour while Kristen and I rappel down to the domes?"

Kristen glared at him in disbelief. "What? You want me to climb out of a perfectly good aircar and slide, what, twenty or thirty meters down a rope? Are you crazy?"

"More to the point," Paul said, "how do you get back up?"

"Uh, a rope ladder. We do have one." He was right, it was the backup for the ship's descent ladder. "Or better yet, a winch. We can dismount the one in the airlock and bolt it to the aircar."

"Or we could fly a bit farther and land in that clearing," Kristen said, pointing at the chart. "And not waste battery power hovering for an hour."

"But it would be the same power consumption as flying that extra distance," Corey said.

"And if you run into trouble on the ground? That raises two problems, getting back up to the car, and extra hover time while you deal with the issue. Besides, somebody has to stay with the aircar while it's in flight, just in case, and I want to check these domes out too." Paul shook his head. "No, we'll go to the farther site. Then our only time constraint on the ground is taking off before it gets dark, if that."

"And if something goes wrong with the aircar? It will be a longer hike back."

Paul couldn't imagine what could go wrong. The vehicle was designed to be highly redundant, and it had been operating fine so far. But Corey had raised a valid concern. "Good point. Let's map out a route to be sure we can walk back. No cliffs or river crossings. I don't think we'll have any problems, the aircar is designed to not be vulnerable to bird strikes, and we could lose two of the six rotors and still fly." Balance would be precarious if those two rotors were adjacent, but the odds of losing even one were minuscule. Aircars were considered nearly as reliable as ground cars. "Anyway, if we do end up having to walk back, you can say 'I told you so.' It's my decision, and we're going to Site B."

∞ ∞ ∞

They flew at five hundred meters above the treetops, having set out at first light that morning. Their altitude was a compromise between being high enough for good visibility, yet low enough to keep well clear of the ever-present clouds of skyweed that tended to rise and fall with the day-night cycle. Corey had been trying to work out how much of that was the sun's—Delta Pavonis's—warmth expanding their gas cells, and how much was sunlight driving the chemical reaction the cells used to generate their lift gas. The day hadn't warmed up enough yet to create the turbulence that would probably plague them on the way back, and Paul took advantage of that to push their speed.

∞ ∞ ∞

195 km NW of landing site

Paul lifted the aircar to 2,500 meters, slightly below the green-tinged cloud deck above them. Below, all he could see were tree-tops. "Where's that clearing? Or, for that matter, the domes? We can't even descend on rope ladders if we don't know where they are."

"Hover here," Kristen said. "Let me take a bearing."

"A bearing on what?" Corey asked. "There's nothing but jungle."

"On the *Verne*," she said. "A radio bearing."

The had followed the heading from the ship on their way out, and they'd come approximately the distance that she had measured on her maps, but any cross-wind could have pushed them away from their desired ground track. A back-bearing on the *Verne* would be a good check.

She took the measurements while Paul held the aircar hovering at altitude. He scanned the jungle, looking for any sign of a clearing, or of any unusual hills sticking above the trees, but the gently rolling terrain defied his attempts.

"Well?" he asked of Kristen as she rechecked her instruments.

"I get a bearing of 114 degrees to the ship, or 294 reciprocal. That's two degrees south of where we should be, so probably a little east, too, if we were fighting a north wind."

"So, a few kilometers northwest, then," Paul said. "Can you give me a heading?"

She ran the calculation on her omni. The numbers were an educated guess but should get them close enough to spot the clearing from the air. "Try 325 degrees magnetic."

They had already established that Verdigris had a magnetic field, and that its north magnetic pole was close to its geographic pole. Maybe the next visitors to this planet would set up navigation satellites.

Paul banked the aircar slightly right as he turned more northward, maintaining altitude. As they cruised over a line of low hills, the color of the vegetation ahead changed, becoming paler and yellower.

"That may be it ahead," Corey said. "Either that's a different kind of tree, or it's affected some way. Maybe a blight or a soil deficiency."

"Or the aftereffect of a small wildfire from lightning strike," Kristen said.

"I see it," Paul said, beginning a gentle descent as he angled toward the discolored vegetation.

A few minutes later, the trees below them thinned out, becoming farther apart, with thinner foliage. While the leaf shapes looked similar to the healthier trees they'd been flying above, the leaves themselves were yellower. Paul slowed their craft, and soon they were above a broad area, perhaps fifty meters across, where there were no standing trees, only a few downed trunks and scattered stumps. He brought the aircar down to below the level of the surrounding treetops, did a few low-level passes before deciding on a reasonably clear, flat area on which to land. Happily, the surface was solid, and not the bog that he had worried the area might turn out to be.

"All right," he said. "Check the immediate area first. What are we going to be walking through? And why is this clearing here at all? Corey, any ideas?"

"Maybe Kristen was right. A fire in the not-too-distant past. The oxygen content *is* higher here than on Earth."

∞ ∞ ∞

They set off toward the nearest dome. From Kristen's aerial radar map, that was roughly a hundred meters into the jungle from the north edge of the clearing. "Clearing" might have been overstating it. While devoid of the typical dense jungle growth, the area where they had landed was still grown high with grass and some scrubby bushes. Paul glanced back toward the aircar and saw a problem. If they went much farther in this, the low, open-framed aircar would be hard to spot amid the surrounding scrub.

"Wait a moment. I need to do something." He shrugged off his small backpack and dug out a few items; a slim metal stake, a small electronics module, and a cylinder the size of a small beverage can. He ran the wires from the module to a connector on the can, then attached the stake to clips in the side of the can and drove it into the ground, leaving the can perched about twenty centimeters above the surface. He stood up, then tapped and swiped the screen on his omni. Satisfied, he nodded. "*Bien*, let's go."

"Is that a radio beacon?" Corey wondered aloud.

"Not exactly," Paul said, grinning. "It's a remotely triggered smoke bomb. It will also emit a loud whistle while burning. We should be able to find our way back to this clearing, at least. This will help us figure out where we parked."

∞ ∞ ∞

The going got tough once they were out of the clearing, with thick underbrush occupying the jungle floor almost as densely as the canopy overhead. It was similar to what they'd encountered nearer their landing site, but at least there they'd had the option of following animal trails, or taking the boat along the river. Here, with a specific target in mind, they were forced to either hack through tangles of vegetation or be forced off their course.

And hack they did. Paul paused to rest after cutting through a particularly recalcitrant thicket, wiping the sap and leaf fragments of the blade of his machete before touching up the edge with a sharpening stone.

"*Merde*," he said, rubbing the sweat away from his brow. "I wish we had brought laser machetes."

"Ha, might as well wish for a light-saber," Corey said.

"No, I'm serious. Something my father's company has been looking at. I've seen mock-ups but no prototypes yet. The problem is the power pack is quite large, and they still have some problems with the beam-stop. Nobody has figured out a way to magically make a light beam stop by itself after only a meter."

"I think a chainsaw would be more practical," Corey said.

"You know, guys," Kristen said, "something's been bothering me. I just realized what it is."

"Oh? What?"

"This jungle is too quiet. Listen." She held up her hand for silence. All Paul could hear was the slight murmur of the wind in the upper branches and the occasional whine of the never-far-away mosquitoes.

After a minute, Corey said, "I don't hear anything. What?"

"Exactly," Kristen said. "Everywhere else we've been, there's been that incessant hooting, the owls or whatever, but—"

"It's not owls," Corey objected. He had been trying since soon after they'd landed to figure out exactly what bird or animal it was, but without success.

"Whatever. Rick's ocarinas, then. I haven't heard it here, not since we landed the aircar."

Corey shrugged. "I guess we're out of its habitat."

"What's different about this jungle versus the others?" she said.

"Its range, then. We have come a couple of hundred kilometers."

"There are also the domes we're looking for," Paul said. "If they're made by some animal, perhaps the not-owls don't like them."

"Or that," Corey agreed. He checked the mechanism on his rifle. The others did likewise.

"Or maybe it's nothing," Kristen said. "We should get moving again."

"*Oui*," Paul agreed. "How much farther?"

"About thirty meters to the nearest. We should be able to see it soon."

They peered ahead through the jungle. There was a darker patch ahead, but Paul couldn't tell if it was merely another thicket or the side of one of the domes. Either way, it was dark and green.

"Okay, let's go." He raised his machete and swung it down on the nearest branch.

Within a few more minutes, the gaps between the tree trunks abruptly widened, although overhead their canopies still overlapped, shielding the view from the sky.

A few meters in front of them, a large mound or boulder rose from the ground, green with moss.

"Is this it?" Paul asked. "It looks like a huge boulder. What's the term? Left by a glacier?"

"An erratic," Kristen said. "No, I don't think so. We would have seen others of different sizes." She stepped forward and scraped at the moss with her machete. It dug in a couple of centimeters, and they heard the muffled scrape of steel upon stone.

Switching out the machete for her geologist's pick, she used its point to scrape a rectangular outline through the moss, about a meter on each side. She pried loose an upper corner, then, like pulling up a carpet, tugged on the mossy layer until it peeled back in a sheet, leaving a thin residue of dirt and roots on the stone behind it.

"So, it is just a big boulder," Corey said.

"*Non, regardez*." Paul had noticed a straight, narrow indentation running vertically along the surface near one side of the stripped rectangle but separate from the scratch marks left by Kristen's pick. He rubbed away the residual dirt from the indentation, revealing a crack or seam in the rock. Excitedly, he knelt and began pulling the moss away from where the seam extended underneath it to reveal another such seam running horizontally. The vertical seam met it at an inverted T, as close to a 90-degree angle as he could tell.

"*Merde*," he said. "That has to be artificial. There's intelligent life on this planet after all."

"Was," Corey said. "We've seen no evidence that there is any still around, and we've been looking. This place has been abandoned for a long time."

"How long? Jungle can overgrow ruins like this in only a few hundred years," Paul said. "Look at Indonesia or the Yucatan."

"This place could have been desert for thousands of years, and the jungle is recent," Kristen said. "Some of those hills we flew over could have been ancient dunes. Corey's right. We haven't seen any current signs of intelligent life. No fields or cleared forests, no villages. Nothing."

Paul let himself be partly mollified. A still-extant civilization could ruin any chances to profit from this planet, depending on what the *UDT* ultimately decided to do about Taprobane and the timoans. Either way, he'd be famous as the explorer who first set foot here. Or it could be that they had indeed gone extinct, like whoever left behind the stone tools on Sawyer's World, or as humans themselves almost had a few times in their history.

"*Eh bien*. We should uncover more of this dome, see what it tells us about whoever built it. And, Kristen, is there some way you can tell how old it is? Some rock test that will say when it was built?"

Corey had already begun working his way around the structure, taking samples of the moss and the small blue flowers growing on it, and any other plants or insects that caught his eye as something he hadn't seen before.

Kristen banged her hammer on the stone surface experimentally, then got out a chisel and knocked off the corner of the block they'd partially uncovered. "I don't know how accurately I'll be able to tell the age," she said, examining the freshly fractured surface. "The stone has weathered on the surface, but I don't know enough yet about how fast it weathers, or even if the weathering rate has been constant. It won't have been, if this place was a desert before the jungle took over."

"Haven't you been building up a geological history of the planet?"

"I have, but it's a very broad picture. It could take years of field-work to get the detail needed to accurately date this."

"You know it can't be millions of years, though."

"No, probably not. I can date the native stone, but that won't tell me when it was quarried and shaped into blocks. There are a few other tests that might tell us something." She peered at the surface of her sample. "Maybe I can find cosmic ray traces. They're more likely to affect the surface at a uniform rate than chemical changes; they won't be affected by climate." She paused and looked up at him. "You know, there *is* still a chance that this is natural. Sometimes stone cracks in ways that look artificial at first, even forming T-junctions."

"Well, that's something. Take as many samples as—"

He was interrupted by Corey's shouts. "Come over here, take a look at this!"

∞ ∞ ∞

Corey was about a quarter of the way around the dome—it was perhaps eight or nine meters in diameter—and bent down against the side, peeling back moss and tossing it haphazardly aside.

"What have you got?"

He stood up, still partially blocking their view of where he'd been digging, and said breathlessly, "I noticed some strange lumps in the moss. I thought it might be roots or something growing under it, so I peeled it back. It wasn't roots. I pulled away more, and, well, look." He stepped aside.

It was only partly uncovered; Corey had called them as soon as he'd realized what he had, but the upper part, what he'd thought was a root, was a raised relief carved into the stone, forming the outside of a circle. Within that, where he'd torn the moss away, were more stone ridges, part forming the upper part of an arch, curving down into the moss, and below and to the side of that, a horizontal oval, surrounding a circle, with a vertical groove bisecting it. An eye, with a slit-pupil, like a snake's.

"Oh," Kristen said. "No, that's definitely not natural."

Chapter 25: Meanwhile at the *Matthew*

Matthew *landing site*

Sebastian Thorne, the *Matthew*'s second in command, found the captain at the folding table set up in the campsite adjacent to the ship. It was still morning there, and Talbot sat drinking coffee with their team's geologist.

"Sir, it looks like the *Verne* crew are visiting their own domes," Thorne told Talbot. "I spotted their aircar in a clearing near one of the sites." The *Matthew* had also left satellites in orbit, both for general survey and to check up on the activities of the rival ship.

"Any differences from the ones we found?" Talbot asked. There had been several near the *Matthew*'s landing site, overgrown and crumbling. It was curious that a place nearly half the world away also had them.

"Not that I can tell. The site may be a little less haphazard than ours. Maybe it's newer."

"No sign of current habitation, though?"

"No more than anywhere else."

"Okay, good." Talbot's team hadn't found any sign that whoever had built the strange stone hemispheres were still around. If there were any signs of cultivation, or pens for animals, they had long been covered by the jungle, or by drifting dunes during the ice age this planet had emerged from a few thousand years ago. All to the good, as far as Talbot was concerned. Sad for the extinct intelligent natives, of course, but he took a philosophical view. Intelligent species had been going extinct on Earth for almost as long as they'd been around; look at the Neanderthals, for example, or whatever came before them. Modern humans had nearly gone extinct themselves a few times, most recently a few decades ago with the Unholy War. If this planet had been left uninhabited, then perhaps those same modern humans could make some use of it, and he'd happily pocket a share of the profits. *If* it were uninhabited, and if the *Matthew* got back to register a claim first.

"We should start wrapping things up here. We've sampled everything locally. We know the place is terraformed."

"But there's still plenty to explore," complained the geologist.

"And it will still be here when we come back, or if we don't, I'll recommend you to accompany whoever does. We'd need to up-ship for you to check out the desert or the ice cap, and frankly neither of those are likely to have much interest to our primary sponsor. When we lift, we're heading back to civilization." As if for emphasis, he slapped at the mosquito just lighting on his arm.

"And I think we'll do that as soon as we can get everything packed up and stowed." He turned to Thorne. "Pass the word."

Chapter 26: The Domes

The dome, Verdigris

It took them a half-hour to strip the moss and other vegetation away from the carving. Paul and Kristen took a few pictures, but the rate at which they tore the covering away would have horrified any archeologist. Fully exposed, it was clearly a face, very alien-looking, yet somehow more mammal than reptile, despite the snake eyes and the shallow nose with thin vertical nostrils. It was the mouth, Paul decided. No reptile had the kind of cheek pouches and lips that formed the great O of a mouth the face had. He wondered whether it was supposed to be yelling or screaming. No, the expression around the eyes belied that, as if this being's expressions could bear any relation to that of a human or even an ape. Perhaps it was hungry.

"What do you think, Corey? Could that be related to any existing animal here, or is it something more abstract, like a god or demon?"

"We've seen the cat-like eyes in other creatures here. On Earth, they'd tend to indicate a small animal, one that lives close to the ground. Here? Who knows? As for the rest, without seeing the body it attaches to, I have no idea. At a guess, I'd say it was probably a good representation of whoever made the dome and carved the image."

"Tell that to the ancient Egyptians," Kristen said. "Didn't they have animal-headed gods?"

Corey shrugged. "You're right. But for what it's worth, we haven't seen any animals with heads that look like that. But it's a big planet."

"They'd be something native to the area, surely," said Paul.

"Back whenever this was built, yes. Now? It could be extinct, or it could have migrated elsewhere."

"So why here? What's this face *for*?"

"Decoration? Are there any others?"

They worked their way around the structure, probing and peeling at the overgrowth at intervals as they went. They found some carvings, mostly abstract—lines, dots, small circles, even a crescent and a few six-pointed asterisks. Corey thought these represented flowers. Paul wasn't so certain—but no other faces.

"Only one face, with a large mouth. Do you suppose it could be an entrance?"

"You think the dome is hollow, like an actual igloo?"

"Why not? If it's a burial chamber or a storehouse, there would need to be an entrance," Paul said. "If the open mouth represents eating, perhaps it's something like a grain store."

Kristen knelt beside the face, poking and prodding at the surfaces, at the narrow gaps around the circles of the mouth and face, even poking into the slit pupils and nostrils with the pick of her hammer. "Nothing," she said, her tone a mix of disgust and frustration. If it is supposed to open, they didn't make it easy."

"After who-knows-how-many hundreds or thousands of years, any mechanism is probably long since corroded or calcified solid," Paul said.

"I could come back with a seismic charge. . . ." Kristen said, half smiling.

Paul wasn't sure she was joking. "The archeologists would kill us," he said. "Let's just take a lot of pictures, and if there's anything *nondestructive* you can do to give us more information about the interior, we'll consider doing that." He checked the time. "But we need to start wrapping up here. I'd rather not fly back in the dark, and I *definitely* want to get back out of this jungle before nightfall."

The others agreed, and fell to photographing the carvings they had uncovered before it was time to leave.

Chapter 27: Last Days on Verdigris

Verdigris, Jules Verne landing site

"Paul, we just got a signal from one of our observation satellites. The other ship just launched," Rick said.

"Does that matter?" asked Mary. "We're almost ready to lift ourselves, and we can prove we landed first."

Paul wasn't so confident. "That proof won't matter if they get back ahead of us and register their claim first. Yes, we might get that overturned, but it would mean a lawsuit. It would drag on and drain our funding. Even then, we might lose. We need to get back before them. How soon can we launch?"

"No less than six hours, by the time we get the *Verne* loaded and buttoned up. If we want to pick up our subsats, another few hours. I need to work out the orbits," said Rick.

"Can we skip that step? Is there any data we haven't downloaded?"

"Well, no, but that's valuable hardware," Rick said.

"But not worth the time. They'll have a half-day lead on us, and they might be faster."

"What if there's a shorter route?"

Paul looked at him, intrigued. "Is there?"

"I'll need to double check, but I've been thinking about it. There are stars closer to here than Epsilon Indi. They won't have terraformed planets, but we can refuel from an ice moon or even a plutoid. We might cut some distance that way."

Paul looked at Mary. "What do you think? Is that feasible?"

"Theoretically," she said. "I've done scenarios like that on the simulators, in case we had to do it here. It's worth looking at, but it will take time to find a refueling spot in an uncharted system."

"*Bien*," Paul nodded decisively. "Rick, investigate that while the rest of us get the *Verne* ready for take-off."

He got on his omni to the others. "Kristen, Corey, we've had a change of plan. Stop what you're doing and gather up all your specimens and data. We have only a few hours to raise ship."

"*What's the rush?*" Corey said. "*I thought we had another two days?*"

"Our friends on the other ship have just departed without the courtesy of giving us notice. We think they're going to jump our claim. If you want your contracts with Skrellan or Galactic Mining to be worth anything, we need to get back before they do."

"*We're already behind, then. What difference will it make?*"

"Rick is looking for a shortcut. If he finds one, we'll need to leave as soon as possible. If not, then it's moot, and you can have a few more days. If there *is* a shortcut, and your dawdling threatens to delay our departure, I may have to leave you here."

"*You wouldn't!*" Kristen said.

"It's terraformed," Paul said icily. "Somebody will be back in a couple of months. Sawyer's group survived for four years." He wouldn't really abandon them if they weren't ready to go, but he wanted to convince them of the urgency.

"*We're on our way back now.*"

∞ ∞ ∞

Aboard the Jules Verne*, a few hours later*

"What do you have for us?" Paul asked Rick.

"Launch windows and trajectories for an orbit to line us up for going to warp. We have several options."

"Have you found a shortcut?"

"That's not looking so good, I'm afraid. Total distance from here to Sol by the route we came is 23.16 light years, call it 21.2 days, plus a refueling stop at each of Epsilon Indi and Alpha Centauri. That's at least another day each, so 23.2 days. We can assume the other ship is headed back that way."

"Okay, and?"

"If we go via the red dwarf Gliese 832, the total trip is 23.5 light years, or 21.5 days, with one fuel stop, so 22.5 days."

"Saving us a bit less than a day. It will be a tight race. Do we know that we can refuel at Gliese 832?"

"It's known to have at least two planets, a Jovian and a super-Earth. The latter is at the outer edge of the habitable zone, and the Jovian is well beyond the frost line. It's almost certain to have ice moons."

"We're screwed if it doesn't."

Rick nodded glumly. "True, and that's not the whole story. From Gliese 832 to Sol is 16.1 light years."

Paul cursed. "That's way beyond our range, even if we use up all our reserves."

"We can store extra deuterium in the hydrogen propellant tanks. We just need to reconfigure some valves. That will do it."

Paul accepted that. The *Verne*'s chemical engines ran on a shifting mix of liquid oxygen, liquid methane, and liquid hydrogen, with tanks for each. The deuterium for the fusion reactors was just another kind of hydrogen, and while it would be wasteful to burn it in a chemical engine, it needed the same cooling and insulation as regular liquid hydrogen. But. . . .

"Don't we need the hydrogen to make orbit?"

"Not all of it. There's a separate header tank for landing reserve. We won't need that for landing on the moon for quarantine."

"So, we use *that* tank for deuterium instead?"

"That's the idea."

"Do we *have* enough deuterium?"

"We won't need it for the first hop, that's only 7.4 light years. We can process extra at Gliese 832."

"*If* the planet has an ice moon. All right, let's run it by Mary."

∞ ∞ ∞

Paul explained the situation to Mary, with Rick filling in some of the details. Finally, she was satisfied with the technical solution. But there was something else.

"Okay, I'll buy that we can probably get to the Solar system before the other guys do. But they'll get to Alpha Centauri before we get to the Solar system."

"So what?" Rick said.

"*Merde*," Paul muttered. "Of course."

"What?" Rick didn't get it. "Why is that a problem?"

"Kakuloa is officially *UDT* territory, despite the Treaty of Alpha Centauri. William Blake is the *UDT* representative. Our friends in the other ship don't have to go all the way to Earth to file a claim; they can—and almost surely will—file it with him first. That date sets precedent, even if we get to Earth before they do, or before Earth even hears of their claim."

"Shit, that sucks."

Mary turned to Rick. "How far to Alpha Centauri by way of Epsilon Indi? 18.86 light years?"

"That's right, why?"

"It's only 16.5 light years from here to Alpha Centauri," she said.

"So what? We can't do that in one jump. A V-class can't do it in one jump either," Rick said. "Fifteen light years is the limit, ten for the older ones."

"A few minutes ago you were talking about doing a 16.1 light year jump from Gliese 832 to Earth."

"Yes, but that's with refueling in space. If we fill a hydrogen tank with deuterium here on Verdigris, it will weigh twice what it should. That's going to throw our mass budget off and reduce the engine performance. We might not make orbit."

Paul thought he saw where this was going. "If we could do it," he said, "would that be enough extra deuterium to get us to Alpha Centauri?"

Rick pulled out his omni and punched in a calculation. "Yes, just barely. And only because our warp system is nearly three percent more efficient than spec."

"I like that idea better than the risk of not being able to refuel at Gliese 832," Mary said.

"How long to refine enough extra deuterium? Maybe we can strip weight out of the ship while we're doing that."

Rick made another calculation. "Here? 39.7 hours, minimum."

"Too long," said Mary.

Paul looked at Rick curiously. "What did you mean, *here*?"

"Using the deuterium-hydrogen ratio in the local seawater. It's richer than Earth's, but not as high as in the outer solar system."

"Really?" Paul didn't know why there was a difference, and right now, didn't care. But if that were also true here . . . "How high is it in the outer reaches of *this* system?"

Rick frowned, puzzled, then his eyes widened as he realized why Paul had asked. "Great question. Let me look up the scans we did on the way in." He linked to the ship's computers and began running queries of the astronomical data they had collected. After a couple of minutes, he let out a low whistle. "It averages twice as high. There's one comet where it's nearly three times, similar to some of the comets in our solar system."

"That would be ice, *n'est ce pas*?"

"Yes. We'd have to melt it. But we have the equipment to do that; we didn't know for sure we'd find water."

"So, we could do it in thirteen hours there?" Paul persisted.

"Plus a couple of hours because we'd be dealing with ice rather than liquid water, plus maneuvering time to get there. It would be faster to do it at one of Zeus's moons."

"And we wouldn't need to worry about stripping weight off the *Verne* to make orbit," Paul said.

"No."

"Then let's do that." He turned to Mary. "Where are we with getting the *Verne* ready to launch?"

"Almost done loading, so long as you're okay with abandoning the aircar and other non-essential gear."

"*Oui*, it's not worth the time."

"In that case, we can start buttoning up in another twenty minutes, then begin the countdown sequence."

Paul paused to consider. What was he overlooking? The trip from here direct to Alpha Centauri was a risk, dependent upon fuel calculations and how well using the reserve tank with deuterium actually worked. There was no reason it shouldn't, if the plumbing was as Rick said, and he should know. They could test that out in short warp hops first. If it didn't look good, they could still reach Epsilon Indi. They might lose out on their claim, unless something happened to the other ship, but they could make it back. It might come down to how long it took the others to tank up in the Epsilon Indi system.

"Rick, how long do you think it will take for the others to refuel on Taprobane?"

"A V-class ship? Not as long as it took us. A day, maybe?"

"They can't refuel on Taprobane after landing here," Mary said. "That would violate quarantine regulations. They'll have to use an ice moon."

"You're right," Rick said. "So at least two days, with extra maneuvering and dealing with the ice."

Paul grinned broadly at the news. That improved their odds. This just might work.

"All right then. Last chance to say goodbye to Verdigris." He looked up at the mottled green overcast. Crazy damned skyweed. He looked forward to seeing stars again.

Chapter 28: Zeus

Delta Pavonis system, near gas giant Zeus

They entered orbit around Zeus, aiming for a rendezvous with an ice moon they had already identified as having 2.6 times the deuterium concentration that the seawater on Verdigris had.

"There's one problem," Mary said. "Like Jupiter, this gas giant has massive radiation belts. We can't stay here long, and especially not out on the surface."

"Look for a place to land here," Rick said, pointing out an area on the moon's far side from the planet, and toward the trailing side of its orbit. "That will have the lowest levels. We should only be here twenty hours."

"Double your dosage of anti-rad drugs too," Paul said. "We have plenty."

"Is it safe to take that much?"

"Safer than the radiation," Corey said. "We could go up to four times for a day or so before the drug starts to have a toxic effect."

"Nice," Mary said.

"Thank Victoria Holmes," Paul said. "She got us a supply of the good stuff. Military-grade, it's not cheap."

An hour and a few orbital mechanics shortcuts later, the *Jules Verne* settled onto an icy plain. The huge gas giant lay below the horizon, but Delta Pavonis, even as a pinpoint, gave plenty of light for them to work by.

∞ ∞ ∞

Rick cursed as he dragged the hoses and cutting head out across the ice, his efforts hampered by the space suit he wore. "Man, and I thought working in the BIGs was a pain. This suit is *stiff*."

Paul, likewise suited up and struggling with the gear, had little sympathy. "You know," he said, "it will be much more flexible if you let the air out."

"Yeah, but then *I'd* be a stiff. No thanks."

Paul looked back at the *Verne*. They'd hauled the gear some fifty meters. "That should be far enough," he said. "We're not going to melt a hole back to the landing gear from here."

Rick turned to see. "You're right. Okay, let's get the heater set up."

The apparatus, specifically designed for refueling on an icy body, was conceptually simple. Melt some of the ice, pump the water back to the ship where the heavy water would be separated out then stripped of its deuterium, while the rest of the water would be heated to steam and piped back out to help melt more ice. The tricky bit was to avoid losing too much to the surrounding vacuum, and to make sure you didn't melt anything that supported the weight of the ship you were refueling. Drilling down into the ice before starting helped.

"You know," Rick said as they were securing the heated wellhead into the hole they had finished boring, "the newer Vanguard-class ships, at least those fitted for exploration, have a robotic attachment for this. Push a button, and a long arm extends out with the drill, heaters, and pumps at the end of it. Much easier."

"Well, it's encouraging to know that our friends will have a much easier job refueling in the Epsilon Indi system. That will save them some time. It doesn't help us."

"Their ship looked older, so it might not have that gear. But don't you think they'll just land on Taprobane to refuel? That would save even more time."

"As Mary said, it would also violate quarantine regulations. Something to keep in mind if they *do* get back first. It might disqualify their claim." Paul tightened the last coupling and stood back to check their work. "However, I will be sure that our *next* ship, if there is one, has such automatic gear. Come on, let's get the tanks filled."

Some hours later, chipping the gear out of the ice so they could stow it, Paul again considered the advantages the newer ships had. He was on the verge of deciding to disconnect the hoses at the ship and abandon the refueling gear—they wouldn't need it again—when the ice finally yielded. Twenty minutes later, they were finally back in space.

Part IV - Homeward

Chapter 29: Return to Alpha Centauri

Orbiting Zeus, Delta Pavonis system

"Are you completely certain this is going to work?" Paul asked Rick, not for the first time. "If we come up even one percent short, we'll end up in interstellar space two light-months from Alpha Centauri. Even if our radios could transmit that far, our life support will have run out before they get our distress call."

"Yes," Rick said, "I've run the numbers a dozen times. Mary has run the numbers more than twice, and her calculations agree with mine." Paul looked at Mary, who nodded. Rick continued, "We have enough deuterium to cover the 16.5 light years from here to Kakuloa, and a little bit extra."

"How little?"

Rick hesitated. "Zero-point-three light years."

"Less than two percent. That's not much of a reserve."

"Eight hours. Aircraft regs only require an hour."

"Aircraft aren't expected to stay in the air for two weeks at a time. Mary, what's the requirement for spacecraft?"

Mary glanced from Paul to Rick and back again. "It's not exactly defined. Spacecraft in normal space only use fuel for delta-vee, so the regs are more in terms of life support reserves. They haven't caught up with warp flight."

Paul sighed. He knew this was the only way to make it back to Alpha Centauri ahead of the other ship, and if he were the only one aboard, he'd risk the jump without hesitation. But he was ultimately responsible for the lives of everyone aboard. They were *also* counting on him to make this trip profitable, which it wouldn't be if they couldn't file their claims first. Paul began to have more sympathy for some of the decisions he'd seen his father labor over.

He looked back at Rick. "You're ready to commit to this?"

Rick nodded. "Yes, the numbers work out. Let's do it."

Paul turned to Mary. "You're the pilot; are you comfortable with it?"

"I don't know if *comfortable* is the word I'd use, but willing, yes. Rick is right about the numbers."

He turned to Kristen and Corey. He paused before asking the same of them. They weren't considered flight crew, but he felt they ought to have a chance to voice their opinion. But what would he do if either of them said no? Give up and take the slow road home? Leave them on Verdigris with a promise to be back for them in a month? Ignore them and take the direct route anyway? What did *he* want? *Merde.* "All right. Kristen, Corey, any thoughts?"

Corey shrugged. "I'd prefer more of a margin, but I'd also prefer to be rich. I didn't expect this mission to be without risk. Hell, the wildlife on Verdigris already tried to kill me twice. If that doesn't convince the rest of you that I'm a jinx, then I'll go along with whatever you decide, Captain."

"*Bon.* Kristen?"

"I'm kind of with Corey. One expects some risk in fieldwork, but on the other hand, I'd rather be alive and poor than dead. Once we go to warp, is there any way to change our minds if things aren't working as expected?"

Paul shook his head. "I don't see how. We can't see where we are while in warp, and once we start, we can't change course. It's like leaping a gap; we can't change our minds halfway."

"That's not quite true," Mary said. "We don't have to commit to the full distance, and we *can* come out of warp early. What if we jump one light year, then check our position against our fuel consumption, like we did on the way out. If the numbers don't work, we change course for Epsilon Indi, or worst case, back here, and refuel?"

"*Quelle bonne idée,*" Paul exclaimed, mentally smacking himself for not seeing the answer himself. He'd known that. Usually there would be no reason to break a trip into multiple hops between stars; it was a waste of time. This was a brilliant compromise. Yes, they'd lose a bit of time while doing the measurements and calculations, but it would give them a chance to correct before any error turned fatal. "Mary, let's make it so. All hands, prepare for warp!"

∞ ∞ ∞

Aboard Jules Verne*, interstellar space*

The ship had been in warp now for twenty-one hours, fifty minutes. At their nominal speed of 400c, in another four minutes and fifty-four seconds, they would have come exactly one light year since leaving the Delta Pavonis system.

Some of the crew had slept; as far as flying the ship went, travel in warp was controlled by the clock, and the ship's automatic systems. But Mary had stayed at the control panel until Paul had ordered her to get some rest. He wanted her alert when it came time to calculate their position.

Rick had been working away at some project of his own, running calculations and doing searches on the ship's library. Paul had thought he was compiling the astronomical data they'd collected in the Pavonis system, but at one point found him reviewing the ship's schematics.

"Is there a problem?"

"No, no," Rick said. "I just had a thought about something hypothetical and was satisfying my curiosity."

"*Bien.*" Paul left it at that. He was too tired to listen to one of Rick's obscure facts of astrophysics or ship design; he had only slept fitfully. As the timer counted down toward when the warp drive shut off, he had the impression that everyone was holding their breath. It was silly, he knew. They were either on track or they weren't, and if not, they could divert with plenty of fuel to spare.

"Two minutes to breakout," Mary announced, then adjusted a control slider. "Dimming the cabin lights." While the warp field was engaged, there was nothing to see out the windows or via the external cameras, but she didn't want the view obstructed by interior reflections.

"Anyone want a betting pool on the over-under of our position?" Rick asked. Everyone had already gathered in the control room, but with the lack of gravity, it wasn't too crowded.

"Not if it will tempt you to fudge the calculations," Corey said, trying but failing to inject humor into his tone.

"*C'est suffice*, that's enough," said Paul. "Everyone will do their jobs. We'll check the data, and proceed from there."

"One minute," from Mary. There was a cover over the "EMERGENCY STOP WARP" switch, which had been unused since they left Earth. She flipped the cover open, and held her hand ready. A second's delay would make a difference of half an AU, nothing compared to the distance they were travelling, but she didn't get where she was by being sloppy.

"Breakout in ten seconds," she said, watching the timer. "Five, four, three, two, one, now." She had just started to press the switch when the stars became visible again through the windows.

"We're here," Rick said, as though nobody else had noticed. "Now to figure out where *here* is."

∞ ∞ ∞

An hour later

"Well," Paul demanded when Mary and Rick had finished their star sightings and calculations, "are we on course? Does our fuel consumption match calculations?"

"We're *really* close," Rick said after checking his numbers a third time.

"Close good, or close bad?" Paul said, then cut to the point. "Can we make it to Alpha Centauri at our current rate?"

Rick looked at his numbers, then back at Paul. "No," he said flatly.

"*Merde!*"

"But we may be able to change our current rate."

Paul and Mary both looked at him like he'd grown a third eye. "What?" Mary said.

"Explain yourself."

"We have six warp modules. Our effective speed in warp varies according to the square root of the number of warp modules. Power is directly proportional to the number. If we turn off two of the warp modules, our speed drops to the square root of four-sixths, or around eighty percent. Our power requirement, thus fuel consumption, drops to four-sixths, or sixty-seven percent. We get a factor of one-point-two-two improvement in light-seconds per liter. It will just take us longer."

Paul looked at Mary for confirmation. She was frowning. "Mary? Is he right?"

"Technically, yes," she forced the words out. "But it's crazy. Even if the systems were wired to allow that—"

"They are," Rick cut in, "although we'll need to pull a couple of circuit breakers and change a configuration file in the flight software."

"—even so," Mary continued, not looking any happier, "eighty percent speed won't get us there ahead of the other ship. More importantly, look what happened to Algernon Brenke and his pilot when they tried messing with warp module configurations."

"What did happen?" Paul asked. He knew Brenke had invented the warp drive, and had later met with some kind of accident, but not the details.

"He discovered artificial gravity while changing the warp field symmetry," Mary said. "The unexpected effect was so strong it killed him and the pilot. Messily."

"There's more to it than that," said Rick. "That was with an odd number of modules active; I'm not proposing that. Also, the modules on his prototype ship were not as carefully balanced as ours are, plus his experimental software had a bug. We're not going to be doing any of that at all."

"Okay, but it's still too slow."

"Is it faster than detouring to Epsilon Indi to refuel?" Paul asked.

Mary tapped the calculations into her console. She didn't look happy with the answer. "Technically, no, it's about eleven hours slower, but that's not counting the day or more to refuel at Epsilon Indi. So, in fact, yes."

That sounded worth it to Paul. "All right then—"

"We can do better," Rick said.

"How?"

"We don't have to run at lower power all the way; we only need to save enough fuel to make sure we can reach Alpha Centauri. We can run on full power partway there, then cut our speed to conserve fuel. I just need to run the numbers for the exact trade-off."

"If we're going to do this," Mary said, "I suggest running at lower power for a while first, to make sure the actual numbers match Rick's calculations. We don't want to come up short again."

"I'm okay with that," Rick said, "but it takes about an hour to make the change from one mode to the other. It's not a matter of flipping a switch."

Paul was acutely aware that every hour, and potentially every minute, could mean the difference between them getting their claim registered first or losing out. It could also mean the difference between getting home or running out of life support somewhere in deep space short of Alpha Centauri. "Very well," he said. "We'll do it that way. Rick, walk Mary through the procedures, then calculate the optimum time at each power setting. With any luck, we can still get to Alpha Centauri before the competition."

∞ ∞ ∞

Alpha Centauri system

The *Jules Verne* emerged from warp in the outer reaches of the Alpha Centauri system, approximately 25 AU from Kakuloa, seventeen days later.

"Do you think we beat them?" Rick wondered.

"It's just possible," Paul said. "They would have had to refuel quickly at Epsilon Indi. We might have as much as a half-day's lead on them."

"Only if they took their time getting in and out of the Indi system," Mary said. "Given their rush to leave Verdigris, I wouldn't count on that."

"We can't do anything about it if they did. Set up a course for Kakuloa. Rick, get ready to transmit our initial data package and claim."

"Roger that."

"Don't forget we need to quarantine at Mahina Nui first," Mary reminded him. "Setting course for there."

"Agreed."

As Mary began pivoting the ship, Paul began sweeping the radio frequencies for whatever information might be available. There was the standard advisory beacon, of course, notifying all ships entering the system to report to UDT space traffic control when within range. They wouldn't be for hours, even with an additional small warp deeper into the system. Space traffic control didn't like ships to suddenly appear before their radio transmissions did, although the Centauri system wasn't yet near as busy as the Solar system.

They were still far enough out that most ship transmissions were so faint as to be nearly lost in the noise, but one came in strongly.

"*Kakuloa Control, this is the ship* Matthew, *inbound from Delta Pavonis by way of Epsilon Indi. Current position is—*" a sequence of coordinates followed. "*We are heading for quarantine at Mahina Nui. We landed on Delta Pavonis III, a terraformed world, and wish to file a claim—*"

"Bastards!" Paul yelled. "And no mention of us at all."

"So that's it then," Rick said. "We're screwed."

"Maybe not," Mary said. "What's the time-stamp on that message?"

It would be encoded in the signal. Paul checked a screen. "Forty-three minutes ago. Why?"

"Their position is a half-light-hour closer to Kakuloa than we are. The wavefront of that signal is still nearly two light-hours from Kakuloa. We can beat it."

Paul understood. If the *Verne* warped into the inner system, they would outrun the *Matthew*'s radio signal, and get their own claim in before the claim jumpers. There were just two problems. "Only if they haven't warped closer in themselves and retransmitted their signal," he said, then held up a hand for silence.

As part of the ship's flight data recording system, the cockpit voice recorder couldn't be shut off while in flight. It could, however, be masked. Paul unwrapped his omni from around his wrist. "Shall we have a little music?" he said, tapping an icon on his omni's screen to provide just that. He slapped it to a stickypad near the CVR microphone.

"What the hell?" Rick asked in a lowered voice.

Paul grinned. "Yes, we can go closer and broadcast our claim, but we violate all kinds of regulations warping in that close."

"We don't have to go 'that close,'" Mary said, "just closer than they do, and those same regs will discourage them from warping in too close. I'll take us out of the main traffic routes."

It was a long shot. Paul knew he could lose the *Verne* if Space Traffic Control wanted to come down hard on them for violating regulations, with no guarantee that the claim would be accepted even if they did beat the claim jumpers. The music would provide plausible deniability as to the exact conversation they were now having.

"You know they could take away your license too, even if I am the one in command?" he asked Mary.

She hesitated. He could see the concern play across her expression. He couldn't imagine what she'd do if she wasn't allowed to fly.

"I'll take that chance."

"I can't let you," Paul decided.

"We're giving up?" Rick said.

"No. Mary, get us lined up. I'll push the button. That puts it all on me."

"Already in position." She had been making adjustments while they talked. "Warp duration of twenty-five seconds, programmed in."

"Thank you." He retrieved his omni and turned off the music. "So, you *can* calculate a jump even with a noisy distraction," he said, winking at her. "Of course, that was just a training exercise," Paul said. "I wouldn't ask you to violate regulations." That was for the cockpit voice recorder.

"Rick, are you ready with that data packet?"

"Affirmative. Ready to transmit on your signal."

"Very well." Paul reached across the control panel, flipped up the cover of the "Engage Warp" button, and pushed it.

As the *Jules Verne* went to warp, Paul said, deadpan, "Oops, wrong button. *Merde*," and then grinned. "*C'est la vie*." The ship dropped out of warp again, and he added to Rick, "I guess you might as well go ahead and transmit that claim."

He turned to Mary. "Seeing as we're so close to Mahina Nui now, you can begin preparations for landing."

Chapter 30: Conflicting Claims

Administrator's Office, Kakuloa

"Sir? We have a situation," Gene Riley said, sticking his head around Administrator Blake's doorway.

"What's the problem?"

"The *Jules Verne* is back in-system. So is the *Matthew*. They're both inbound for landing at the Mahina Nui quarantine facility."

"I'm glad the *Verne* made it. So why is this a problem?"

"They've both broadcast discovery claims on the same planet, Delta Pavonis III."

"Who was first?"

"Well, that's the thing, sir. We received *Verne*'s claim first, but from the message headers, it looks like the *Matthew* transmitted first, but from farther out."

"Oh, for. . . ." Blake muttered in disgust. There had to be a story there. The coincidence in timing was just too . . . coincidental. *UDT* law on the matter, such as it was, held that the claim went to the first to file—but the law hadn't caught up with issues of non-simultaneity in a universe where faster-than-light travel was a thing. That meant it would be up to him to make a decision as to what *first* meant, one that would probably be appealed anyway. *Why did I take this job?* Blake wondered, not for the first time.

"All right," he said. He would have to talk to both crews and examine the ships' logs. He could conduct his investigation from the comfort of his office on Kakuloa, but the radio delay would make that frustrating. Being there in person would also allow the opportunity for some off-the-record conversations.

"They're *both* planning to quarantine?" he asked Riley.

"Yes, sir."

"Then they both landed on the planet. But they'll be stuck on Mahina Nui for two weeks." Blake sighed. "Okay, I don't want to try dealing with this over a comm-link. Clear a few days out of my schedule and arrange transportation. I'm going to have to go up and sort this out in person."

"Already on it, sir."

Of course he was. It was like Riley could read his mind. Well, it was a chance to get off-planet. Blake sighed again. "I hope whatever they found is worth the trouble."

Thus, he would find himself, together with the crews of the *Jules Verne* and the *Matthew*, in a cramped conference room on Kakuloa's larger moon, part of the quarantine facility that, as he himself had emphasized, was a mandatory stop for any ship arriving from other than Earth or Sawyer's World. *What fun.*

∞ ∞ ∞

Mahina Nui Quarantine Facility, Alpha Centauri

Mahina Nui, the larger of Kakuloa's two moons, was much like Earth's own moon, a barren rocky ball big enough to be considered a planet if it were alone in its orbit around its star. Its quarantine facility was also similar to the one on Luna, but smaller. In addition to modest accommodation for ship personnel, it had a biology lab and a sick bay. So far, neither had been needed to counter any virulent organisms brought back from a newly discovered planet. Apparently, sixty-five million years of isolation was sufficient to ensure that diseases evolved for species of one planet were too specialized to infect those of another. But neither the *UDT* nor Centauri Pharmaceuticals were ready to assume that would always hold true; the risks were too high.

The facility also had conference rooms, and it was in one of these that William Blake, along with the captains and pilots of the *Jules Verne* and the *Matthew*, was growing increasingly frustrated with the discussion.

"We seem to have a bit of a problem," Blake said. "You're both claiming discovery rights to Delta Pavonis III."

"I don't see the problem," Paul Fabron said. "We landed on the planet first, and you received our claim first."

"Only because you broke regulations and warp jumped deep in-system to transmit that claim," Ed Talbot shouted. "We transmitted our claim first; the timestamp proves it."

"But we were already on the surface when you got there! We landed first!" Mary Kalvak shouted back.

"Prove it! Anyway, by law the claim goes to the first to register."

"Then it goes to us!" Paul said. "Our claim was received first!"

"But the *Matthew* transmitted first!"

Blake slammed his hand down on the table with a bang. "Enough!" he bellowed in a tone he hadn't used since his military days. "Out here, the law is what I say it is, although you're free to appeal that to the *UDT* courts on Earth." Blake knew he exaggerated about his word being law, but only a little, and his statement had the desired impact. Both parties shut up.

"I'm commandeering the logs from both your ships. They will be reviewed with particular attention to who, when, and where. A report, along with my recommendation, will then go to the *UDT* Space Exploration Council on Earth, and they will make a final decision."

"But—"

"I'm not done. I will remind you that, the Treaty of Alpha Centauri notwithstanding, there is nothing in the Outer Space Treaty that provides for exclusive claim on an entire planet. *Especially* not if the planet has intelligent natives, like Taprobane, for example."

"Verdigris doesn't," Paul interjected. "They're extinct. Just like Sawyer's World. The ruins we found must be thousands of years old."

"And you searched the whole planet for descendants of that culture, did you?" Blake said, raising a skeptical eyebrow.

"Well, not on the ground," Paul said. "But from orbit, we didn't see any signs of them."

Talbot nodded and added, "We didn't see any sign signs of intelligent natives on *New Ireland*—to give the planet its proper name—either." He emphasized the name with a glare at Paul. "We saw ancient ruins, overgrown and decaying, but no natives."

"Well, at least there's something you two can agree on. That's progress, I suppose, although it's in both your interests to agree on that."

He paused, surveying the conference table, as if daring anyone else to speak. Nobody did.

"All right," he continued. "You can all return to your quarters. I may have more questions later."

∞ ∞ ∞

As the others filed out of the conference room, Blake brought up the maps of the green planet. Verdigris or New Ireland, depending on who had actually landed first. The two ships had landed on different continents, which suggested to Blake a solution.

The more he thought about it, the better he liked it. Shortly after Columbus's first voyages to the Americas, hadn't the Pope divided the world along a meridian of longitude, assigning part to Spain and the other to Portugal? Blake did a quick computer search. If he could find a precedent. . . .

He hadn't remembered it exactly right, but close; the 1494 Treaty of Tordesillas had granted a bit more to Portugal than Pope Alexander VI's earlier decree had. And, while the situation confronting Blake was different, the Tordesillas treaty *was* a precedent, and *UDT* bureaucrats loved their precedents; it gave them someone else to blame for their decisions. He would mention it in his recommendations.

And speaking of recommendations, what *about* possible natives? Blake pondered the situation. The natives on Taprobane were clearly intelligent and widespread, with a roughly iron-age civilization. The UDT had decided on a mostly hands-off policy there, only allowing limited, controlled contact. Whoever had left the stone tools and weapons found on Sawyer's World had apparently died out over a hundred thousand years ago. The ruins these two crews had found, at widely separated areas on their planet, suggested that there had been one or more neolithic civilizations there much more recently.

Had they really gone extinct? Civilizations could collapse, sure, and perhaps a global ecological catastrophe had led to that. Could the advent of skyweed have wiped out their agriculture? It wasn't Blake's field; the archeologists and ecologists would have to work it out. But wouldn't some of the natives have survived? Surely, they could have adapted? He shrugged. None of the ships' orbital surveys had shown any signs of recent agriculture. If there were descendants of the builders still around, they had fallen a long way. Without concrete evidence of current intelligent natives, Blake doubted the planet would be declared off-limits, especially not if it held valuable resources, but either way, the decision was far above his pay grade.

He closed the file. That was fine with him. He had enough problems on Kakuloa without worrying about the rest of the terraformed worlds in space.

Chapter 31: Heading Home

Earth's Moon, Quarantine Station

The crew of the *Jules Verne* had been on Luna a week now. Between that, the days in transit from Alpha Centauri, and the time they had already spent quarantined on Mahina Nui—they hadn't set foot on Kakuloa on the return trip—they were now clear to proceed to Earth, via commercial shuttle.

"What's going to become of the *Verne*?" Rick wondered as they finished packing.

"It stays here," Paul said. "It can't return to Earth without being thoroughly decontaminated and sterilized. That eventually happened with the *Chandrasekhar*, since it's a historic ship, but I don't see the point with the *Verne*. It can stay here on the moon, although it would be nice if someone would take it off our hands. I'd rather not have to keep paying parking fees."

"I could fly it to a crater over the horizon," Mary said. "No parking fees there."

"*Oui*, but how would you get back? Walk?" Paul asked. "Anyway, we don't want someone to come along and claim it as salvage. I'd rather sell it, if possible."

"Aren't we going to use it again?" Rick asked. "I thought we were going back?"

"Don't you have classes to finish? Anyway, it's not the most practical ship for such voyages. I would rather trade up to a V-class. I also have some ideas for a side trip."

"Oh? Where to?"

"It was partly your suggestion. V-class ships can't pull the same trick of extending their range by shutting down warp pods, can they?"

"No, not easily. They only have three warp modules, more powerful than what we have in the *Verne*, but the symmetry is wrong. So?"

"*Eh bien*, let's assume the Epsilon Indi system is declared off-limits altogether. How does one get to Delta Pavonis with a fifteen light-year range limit?"

"Uh," Rick consulted his omniphone. "Oh! By way of Gliese 832, it's less than fourteen light years from Alpha Centauri. But that's assuming there's a place to refuel there."

"*Précisément*. I propose we go take a look, and perhaps set up a refueling station there."

"That sounds rather ambitious," Mary said. "Are you expecting much traffic?"

Paul smiled. "I've been spending some of our quarantine time examining star charts. Delta Pavonis is a strategic location. It's less than fifteen light-years from both Beta Hydri and Zeta Tucanae, each a single G-type star, as well as from two binaries with K-type stars—"

"So potentially four more terraformed planets," Rick cut in.

"Yes, and two more star systems after that when they get the range up to sixteen light-years."

"And when, exactly, would we make this trip? As you said, we have classes. Winter break won't be nearly long enough."

"No, it wouldn't. One option would be to take a semester off."

"If class scheduling permits," Rick said. "Not likely with fourth-year courses."

"There's a lot to be done first anyway, including settling the claims over Verdigris." Neither side had been happy with William

Blake's proposed solution, and while both agreed it was better than nothing, final resolution would be up to the courts. At least Paon Co. would get something up front. Paul had very good lawyers to write up Paon Co's contracts, so they would receive finder's fees even while the royalty claims were being decided.

"How long will that take?"

"These sorts of cases can typically drag on for years," Paul said, "but that will largely be up to the various clients that we and the *Matthew* contracted out to. With any luck, they'll come to a mutually acceptable compromise before they spend too much money on lawyers."

"At least you get the naming credit," Mary said. Blake had confirmed, by examining both ships' logs, that the *Jules Verne* had landed first, and that Paul Fabron had made the first footstep.

"*Oui*, there is that," he agreed, and grinned. "Well worth it for the reaction my father had when he found out the name."

"I hope he wasn't mad enough to sell the house," Rick said. "We *will* have somewhere to live when we get back to Kingston, won't we?"

Paul laughed. "Don't worry. I think overall, he was pleased by our venture. He admitted that I must have learned more than I would have at a desk in one of his branch offices."

"I think we can all say that," Mary said. "Boring as it was confined to a ship for weeks at a time, I learned a lot."

"I almost wish I were back in grade school," Rick said.

"What? Why?"

"It used to be something of a traditional assignment to write an essay the first week back. I would love to see the look on the teacher's face if I wrote up our expedition as 'How I Spent My Summer Vacation.'"

Chapter 32: Epilog

Kingston, Ontario

Rick McDonald dumped the rest of his backpack out onto his bed at the house on Alfred Street. He'd already partially unpacked. What remained was mostly destined for the laundry. At least it didn't stink—everything had gone through mandatory radiation or ethylene oxide sterilization upon entering quarantine.

He went through the pile of dirty clothing, not so much sorting it as checking the pockets. That's when he found the odd piece of ceramic that he barely remembered picking up. He thought back. It had been on Verdigris; he'd noticed it on the beach. Then what? Right, that had been when Corey had been attacked by the ROUS, and the alarm raised that he would need medical attention. He'd pocketed the fragment and forgotten about it in the excitement. The bush shirt still had bloodstains on it.

The fragment was curved, like part of a clay bottle or jar, but with several holes that were clearly part of the original object. It was obviously artificial, and must have been made by whoever had built the stone domes they'd found. Except, he'd found it nowhere near one of those sites, and if it were as old as those, surely it would have been buried more deeply, or broken to smaller fragments.

He tried to visualize what the rest of it might have looked like. From the curve, it would have been the size of a potato or a small gourd. He held it in his palm, imagining the whole thing. Almost without thinking, his fingers lined up on the holes, and Rick shivered at the realization, and the memory of the incessant hooting. *Just like an ocarina.*

END

Paul Fabron's story will continue in *Delta Pavonis: Expansion*, coming soon.

For more about what is happening elsewhere on Kakuloa, including William Blake's challenges with Perry Cohen's resort construction and trying to keep tree squids out of the planet's valuable squidberry crops, see the Kakuloa series, beginning with *Kakuloa: A Rising Tide*, available now.

Set several decades later, the Carson & Roberts series opens with archeologist Hannibal Carson hacking his way through the Verdigris jungle looking for a very particular stone structure, in *The Chara Talisman*, and continues from there.

Glossary

Alpha Centauri: closest star system to ours, at 4.3 light years distance. Comprises 3 stars, A, B, and C, respectively of type G (yellow), K (orange), and M (red dwarf). Alpha Centauri C is also called Proxima Centauri.

AU: astronomical unit - the average distance between the Earth and the Sun, approximately 93 million miles or 150 million kilometers

Delta Pavonis: a G type (yellow) star similar to our Sun, 19.9 light years away. Known (as of 2021) to have at least one Jupiter-type planet.

Epsilon Eridani: a K type (orange) star slightly cooler than our Sun, 10.5 light years away. Known to have an asteroid belt and at least one planet.

Epsilon Indi: a K type (orange) star slightly cooler than our Sun, 11.8 light years away. Known to have at least one distant brown dwarf companion, and believed to have at least one planet.

Gliese 832: a red dwarf star about 16.2 light years from Earth. Known to have at least two planets.

Kakuloa: Alpha Centauri B II - terraformed planet orbiting the second largest star (B) in the Alpha Centauri system.

max-Q: Maximum dynamic pressure, the point during a spacecraft launch when speed and atmospheric density combine to exert maximum drag.

multituberculate: an extinct group of mammals which lived on Earth from about 160 to 45 million years ago, notable for a massive, blade-like lower premolar.

omni: Short for omniphone - compares to today's smartphones as smartphones compare to walky-talkies. (Look for "Nokia Morph" on YouTube for a nearly-there concept video.)

omniphone: See omni.

parsec: A distance of approximately 3.26 light-years.

Sawyers World: Alpha Centauri A II - second planet orbiting the largest star (A) in the Alpha Centauri system, the first extrasolar planet settled by humans. (See the Alpha Centauri series.)

Taprobane: Epsilon Indi III - Third planet orbiting Epsilon Indi, home world of timoans.

timoan: (Analogous to "human") The sentient natives of Taprobane. Descended from the ancestral species of terrestrial mongoose and meerkats the way humans are descended from the ancestral species of monkeys or lemurs.

T-space: Terraformed (or Terraform) space - Usual term for "known space," a spheroid of stars centered on Earth and about 20 parsecs in diameter. So-called because many of the sun-like stars within it were found to have planets that were not merely Earth-like, but deliberately terraformed.

Unholy War: A nuclear war which took place in the first half of the 21st century, involving primarily the smaller nuclear powers, purportedly for religious reasons.

Union de Terre: Union of Earth, the successor to the United Nations formed after the events of and immediately after the Unholy War.

Verdigris: Delta Pavonis III - third planet orbiting the star Delta Pavonis, so named for its greenish hue and the heavy jungle covering the habitable areas.

warp bubble: The thin shell of highly-curved space surrounding a ship in FTL flight. Based on Van Den Broek's lower-energy configuration of an Alcubierre warp metric.

Acknowledgments

The inspirations for this book came from several sources. Enthusiastic reader reaction to my *Alpha Centauri* trilogy suggested that other stories about the initial exploration of the terraformed worlds of T-Space might also be well received. Several writers in the Colorado Authors League thought I should try my hand at a Young Adult novel; technically, this misses some of the tropes expected in YA, but the protagonists are definitely young adults. General inspiration came from, among many others, Robert A. Heinlein's classic *Rocketship Galileo* and Steven Gould's thoroughly enjoyable *Wildside.*

Thanks, as usual, to Jill for her valuable feedback in the editing stage, as well as to author Robert G. Williscroft, likewise. Thanks also to my aspiring-paleontologist son Robert for his bringing *Taeniolabis*—a very real, if extinct, multituberculate "rodent" of unusual size—to my attention, and for taking valuable time away from working on his master's thesis to review the final manuscript.

I try to get the details correct in my writing (hard SF authors do the math), but sometimes mistakes slip through. Like any experienced software engineer, I blame the computers.

-- *Alastair Mayer, Colorado, 2021*

About the Author

ALASTAIR MAYER was born in London, England, and moved to Canada with his family as a young boy. He describes his interest in space flight and science fiction as genetic: his father, Douglas W.F. Mayer, had been an early member of the British Interplanetary Society as well as a science fiction fan (who in fact published some of Arthur C. Clarke's first tales in *Amateur Science Stories*).

After attending school in Canada, Alastair became involved in both the L5 Society (now the National Space Society) and computers, publishing articles in *Byte*, *Final Frontier*, and other magazines, as well as becoming an accomplished scuba diver and a private pilot. In 1989 he moved to Colorado, where he still lives, and now writes full time.

His short stories have been published in several anthologies and his work has appeared often enough in *Analog Science Fiction* magazine to gain him entry to the "Analog MAFIA" (Members Appear Frequently In *Analog*). Many of his short works can be found in e-book format on Amazon, Barnes & Noble, Smashwords, and other e-book vendor sites.

Delta Pavonis: Discovery is his 10th novel. It takes place after the events of the *Alpha Centauri* trilogy, and concurrently with *Kakuloa: A Rising Tide.*

Visit his web site at www.alastairmayer.org. Join my email list at www.alastairmayer.net

Subscribers get publication announcements and occasional bonuses. Email addresses are only used as above and never sharedSee my blog at www.alastairmayer.org, which also links to the T-Space Wiki.

Other books by Alastair Mayer

Mabash Books hardcover and trade paper editions are available through your favorite bookseller.

The T-Space™ series comprises:

The Alpha Centauri Trilogy:	ISBN
◦ *Alpha Centauri: First Landing*	978-153-913229-5
◦ *Alpha Centauri: Sawyer's World*	978-154-691328-3
◦ *Alpha Centauri: The Return*	978-197-403548-9

The Kakuloa Series:	Hardcover ISBN
◦ *Kakuloa: A Rising Tide*	978-1-948188-067
◦ *Kakuloa: The Downhill Slide*	978-1-948188-210*
◦ *Kakuloa: Crash and Burn*	978-1-948188-234*
◦ *Kakuloa: The Tide Turns*	978-1-948188-258*

The Carson & Roberts Series:	Hardcover ISBN
◦ *The Chara Talisman*	978-1-948188-081
◦ *The Reticuli Deception*	978-1-948188-104
◦ *The Eridani Convergence*	978-1-948188-128
◦ *The Centauri Surprise*	978-1-948188-173
◦ *The Pavonis Insurgence*	978-1-948188-197

* forthcoming

Ebook editions are also available.

Printed in Great Britain
by Amazon